MIAMI
Heat

TRESSIE LOCKWOOD

AMIRA PRESS

Miami Heat

Amira Press
Charlotte, NC
www.amirapress.com

Chapter One

Sakura set the phone aside and stood to walk around the coffee table. Earlier she had rolled out an exercise mat in the middle of the floor and prepared to do some stretching, but calls interrupted the plan. Work often waylaid her, which meant she'd yet to complete the area she'd chosen as a workout room. Of course, she wouldn't do the redesign herself. She had the means to hire a contractor, but she needed to supervise, and back-to-back travel made that impossible.

"Sakura? Are you still there?"

She sighed and raised her hands over her head in a long stretch, then bent over to press her forehead to her shins. "I'm here, Dad. Just—"

"Am I on speaker? You know I don't like being on speaker, sweetheart."

She rolled her eyes but didn't respond.

"I don't see why you're going to Miami," he complained. "There are plenty of leads for shifters in various other places."

"Are you going to launch into another speech about how great Roger, the new guy, is? I've heard it. He's brilliant. He recovered tons of data from what Shiya dumped, right?"

Her father harrumphed over the line. She pictured his face, scowling, temper rising. Sakura knew how far to push the man before he blew, and she treated him with kid gloves—her dad and her brother, for that matter. They all respected her dad as head of the family and powerful leader of the Keith shifter hunters, but she also recognized how her dad felt about her and her sisters.

Anticipating his reprimand, she continued. "I'm taking a small break, Dad. No big deal."

"Miami though? Honey, there are many exotic locations you could enjoy for your vacation. If it's a matter of money…"

"Please." She chuckled. "The last thing a Keith needs is money." Her father didn't understand the more he protested her flying to Miami, the more she desired to go. She'd been honest about her travel plans but not her reasons. Shae's call took her by surprise, and at first Sakura intended to ignore it and seek out Shiya in Juneau to set her stupid sister straight. Shae, not even being human anymore, was a lost cause, and Sakura still wrestled with whether to fly to Tokyo to hunt her and her lover down. However, when Shae arrived in Tokyo, she had faxed Sakura the picture of their mom, one she'd seen a few times when their brother, Kasen, tried to shove it down their throat as motivation to do their job. Sakura had kicked him in the throat and dared him to try that crap with her again.

When she took the time to examine the picture, along with reading her sister's message, she came to the same conclusion Shae had. Something wasn't right, and she needed to get to the bottom of it. She could simply go to her dad and ask him straight out about what really happened to their mother, but if he were willing to come clean in the first place, they wouldn't be wondering what happened. Now that she considered it, she had no idea why they believed him in the first place. Then again, what reason would she and her sisters have had to think he would lie?

Five years ago, when she got the news her mother was dead, killed by a shifter, she had abandoned her assignment at the time and come home, devastated just like the others. Grief-stricken, they had stood together at her mother's funeral. She remembered she hadn't wanted to go on, didn't think it was possible, but she had hidden it from the others. Shae had been enraged just like Kasen, and Shiya had disappeared behind her computer screen, determined to root out the enemy. Eventually, Sakura found her strength and renewed her dedication to ridding the earth of the unnatural beasts.

Now, she'd been studying the picture of her mother lying in a hotel room bed, her body in tatters. They had blamed the bear shifter all this time, whoever he was. Shae's lover, a cop, had said the wounds were not made by a bear, but she had no intention of going by his word alone. The one fact she did accept after verifying it was that the bridge in the background was located in Miami, not Vegas. That much made it clear things were not as they seemed, and who knew, maybe her dad was in the

3

dark as much as she was about what really happened to her mother. Whomever had been the cause of her losing the woman she had idolized and loved more than life itself, they would answer to her.

"Daddy," she said, placating the man, knowing he'd have kept all three of the girls in pigtails and patent leathers if he could, "it's just for a little while. Don't sweat it. And if Miami turns out to not be the place for me, then I'll fly to…somewhere…maybe Madrid."

Her father sighed over the line. "Okay, honey. One of the men should go with you to keep you safe."

"I'll be fine."

"I'd feel better if—"

"Okay, I'll ask Adam." Her heart sped up with just the mention of the man's name. Adam was her protector and her current lover. She didn't mind him tagging along. Over the last few months, they'd hardly been apart.

"Good," her dad said, and she heard relief in his tone. "Call me when you're settled in."

"Will do. Bye."

She straightened from a lunge and walked over to tap the disconnect button on her phone. Right away, a sound caught her attention, a creak in the floor. Rather than look toward the hall, she pretended not to hear it. Every muscle in her body tensed, but she forced herself to stay loose. Although she strained, she heard no new sound, but she was no longer alone in the house.

Sakura reached for her hairband and pulled her hair back behind her head. With a few twists, she had secured it into a ponytail and rolled her shoulders. When the attack came, she was ready for it. The man leaped over the back of the couch from behind her. She gave him credit for her not seeing him enter the room. At the last second, she sidestepped, and he went hurtling past. He shoulder rolled and landed on his feet, eyes narrowed and trained on her. Sakura took in his build, six feet or a bit over, muscular, short black hair, translucent brown eyes, and a firm jaw.

Before he could move again, she pulled the knife from beneath the couch cushion and hurtled it at him. The man ducked, and the weapon sliced into the far wall at the level where his face had been seconds earlier. His brows rose, but she spun away to retrieve another knife, taped beneath the coffee table.

"Oh no you don't," he groused, his Latino roots clear in the lilt to his words. "You are not getting away from me, *mami.*"

His arm came around her waist, and before she could stomp on his foot, he hauled her off her feet. She elbowed him in the side, and his grasp loosened. A fist to his chin sent his head snapping back, and she broke free, dropped to the floor, and swiped a leg out to trip him. His stance was so strong, her kick did nothing but send vibrations of pain up her leg She gritted her teeth. The attacker wrapped her ponytail around a large fist and brought the bulk of his body down on top of her, pinning her to the floor. Sakura gasped.

"Bastard," she growled, and tried to jab two fingers into his eyes. He caught the hand and jerked her arm across her body. She tried again, but he released her hair and caught that hand, too. Now she lay beneath him, her arms crossed over her head and completely at his mercy. He shifted to hold both wrists in one palm, and then his hips rose off hers. She prepared for another move, but the clink of his belt brought her up short. The next instant, he snatched the seat of her panties aside and sank his cock deep into her pussy. Sakura cried out.

"Mm," he moaned in her ear. "You feel so good. Do you see how hard you made me, fighting me like that?"

Sakura bit her lip and shut her eyes. She stopped struggling and let her forehead rest on the exercise mat. "Adam, you bum, you play dirty."

He chuckled and kissed her ear. "I think I deserve a lot more than this. You didn't hold back with that knife."

"That's my job." She moaned. His deep thrusts drove her insane. The feel of his shaft inside her, combined with his natural male scent, the hardness of his muscles, his voice, all of it worked together to give her ultimate pleasure. This reaction was one reason she hadn't sent him packing like she'd done with past lovers. None of them compared to Adam, but she refused to admit it to him. Let the man think he could be replaced today or tomorrow.

He released her wrists and brought his hands down to her waist. A swift movement rolled him to his back and her straddling his hips with her back to him. Sakura gripped his thighs and began riding his cock.

Her security system was rock solid, and when the alarm didn't go off, she'd known it was him who entered the house. They played these games almost from day one when she began sparring with him, but more and more the fighting led to hot sex. What pleased her just as much as having him make love to her was knowing she could no longer best him. He was right. She'd tried to get the upper hand and bring him down, but somewhere along the way, the greenhorn her dad had brought on to work with the Keith family had grown beyond what anyone ever expected. Sakura hated admitting it, but even with her own dirty tricks to win a fight, she found it impossible to beat Adam. He both frustrated and turned her on.

Adam sat up behind her and brought a hand around her belly. His splayed fingers teased her flesh, making her hotter. She trembled on top of him, desperate to come. When he grabbed her hand and curled her fingers around her panties, he spoke a harsh command in her ear. "Hold them."

She did as he asked, keeping the panties out of the way while he squeezed her waist in a tight hold and drove her up and down his shaft, at the same time pushing upward into her pussy. She screamed his name and rocked hard on him, wanting it all. Her clit throbbed, and she rubbed it, sending sensations of pleasure pulsing through her core. Adam swore in Spanish, and just as she came, shaking and moaning, he emptied himself inside her.

"*Ay, tù tan caliente,*" he murmured, and she fell back against his chest.

She climbed off him and headed down the hall, stripping as she walked. Adam's light step sounded behind her, and she smiled. "You're sloppy, Adam Michael Martinez. I heard you in the hall. You're supposed to be stealthier than that."

"All three names, huh?" he asked, amused. "If your house wasn't so old…"

She glared at him over her shoulder. He'd stripped as well, and she almost missed a step taking in the rich, taut skin that made him look like he had a year-round tan. Adam's knowing glance, his brow raised, said he knew the affect his body had on her. She turned away quickly. One thing she'd learned over the years was never to let a man get control. Not real control, anyway. She didn't mind Adam ordering her sometimes when it came to sex, but that was as far as she'd ever let it go. Loving Adam would mean weakness, and that wasn't happening.

They showered together, Sakura riding him once more while he held her up in front of him. Then they dressed and returned to the living room. She figured she wouldn't get any more exercise in that day, so she rolled up the mat. Besides, Adam had given her more than enough.

"I'm going to Miami," she announced when she was done. "Want to tag along?"

He dropped on the couch, his shirt still open. She resisted going over to sit on his lap or at his side and took an armchair instead. "The thing with your parents?"

"My mom, yes." She eyed him. "You haven't told anyone, have you?"

"Of course not. I'm still reeling from the fact that you shared the details of your concerns in the first place. Sakura Keith doesn't open up easily. I'm going to enjoy it while it lasts."

"Whatever. Anyway, do you want to come along? I told Dad I'd take a protector."

"I'm your only protector," he said, and she smirked. He patted the chair beside him. "Come here."

She raised an eyebrow at him.

"Please."

She sighed and stood to move to his side. When he raised his arm, she gave in to the urge to settle into his side and breathe in his scent. He smelled of her bath gel and shampoo. She pushed fingers into his damp hair, loving how he kept it cut short, almost as if it had been hacked off in stunted spikes, but with order and sexiness.

"Marry me, Sakura."

All thoughts of his hair fled her mind. "Adam, you've asked me a million times…"

"Twice."

"Well, this makes the third time." She straightened. "And don't say that charm thing, or I'll punch you."

He opened his mouth to say something, but changed his mind. A stubborn set she recognized came over him. She saw it in the light in his eyes and the stiffness in his jaw. "I'm not giving up on you."

"You might as well, because it's not happening!" She considered cutting off their relationship, but the words to dump him locked on her tongue. Instead, she tried another tactic to drive the message home. "I helped refine your skills when you were a newb."

"So what?"

"I can't see you as anything, but…well…"

"Beneath you," he growled and surged to his feet.

"You think I'm not on your level because I work for your dad and because when we met you put me on my back with a well-placed kick. Is that it?"

"I don't think you're beneath me."

He bent almost in half, standing in front of her. "Look me in the eyes and say that."

She waved a hand and stood. Pushing him back both failed and turned out to be a mistake. Touching Adam at any time woke desire in her body, even if they'd just had sex, and the man's strength far exceeded her own. She tried moving away. He caught her and spun her to face him.

"Sakura."

Damn, how she enjoyed her name on his lips. She'd always hated the name, feeling it did not define who she was. With the way Shae lived now, with a Japanese lover, the name Sakura would be perfect for her.

"Okay," she admitted. Maybe she needed to offend Adam to make him back off. "I do think you're beneath me. I mean you're right. I can't beat you anymore, but all I still see is the scrawny little weakling that came along begging my father to give him a chance."

Adam flinched. She'd lied. He branded his image on her mind and body on a daily basis. A scrawny weakling was not what she saw.

"You're still begging, but now it's me you want. You already got the job."

His nostrils flared, and he released her to step back. "That's what you think, huh? I'm using you?"

Regret tightened in her chest. "I didn't say that. Look, Adam. We're not right for each other, okay? The sooner you accept it, the better." She dared look at him but didn't see the hurt she expected. His face a mask of anger, his nostrils flared, he spun away to pace. Sakura straightened her shoulders. "Are you going with me to Miami?"

"No."

She blinked. "What?"

He stopped pacing and faced her. She still couldn't read his expression or what might be on his mind. "You said yourself this isn't work related, and I'm just a protector, correct? I'm under no obligation to join you."

"Are you for real? You're going to be that way?"

"What way, Sakura? Did you expect me to trot along behind you, to kiss your ass?"

Her temper flared, and she raised a hand to smack his face, but he caught it. They eyed each other in silence for a few minutes, and then she wrenched her arm from his hold. "You're free to get the hell out of my house."

As she stomped down the hall, she waited for him to follow or to call after her, but his steps echoed in the opposite direction. Soon the front door opened and closed, and Sakura found a tear running down her face. She swiped at it, scrubbing her cheek until it hurt and then began packing a suitcase. From this moment on, she needed to dismiss Adam from her thoughts and concentrate on gathering information about her mother's death. When she returned to San Diego, she and Adam would talk.

Chapter Two

Adam left Sakura's house with myriad emotions storming out of control. She had rejected him again. He'd expected it, of course, but that didn't negate the fact that it tore him up inside—just like the two times before. His biggest issue lay in knowing Sakura loved him. She knew it. He knew it. However, Sakura believed giving in to love meant opening herself to being weak. No one knew the woman as he knew her, and he could say without reservation none of the Keith women were as vulnerable as she was. The difference with Sakura was half her battles were in keeping the wall erected between herself and those around her—including her family. Still, if she thought he intended to give up on the two of them, the sexy little thing was starkly wrong. Sakura would be his and his alone, no matter what he had to do.

For now, he had pissed her off. He knew that. Sakura might push him away, but she expected him to follow her wherever she went, to be her trained puppy, who basked in whatever crumbs of affection she offered him.

Sometimes, like now, he needed to remind her she craved him just as much as he did her, and while she was his Queen, he was her King, and she needed to respect him as such.

He grinned as he pressed heavy on the Maserati's gas pedal. "*Me perteneces*, beautiful lady. You are mine. Just a matter of time."

Adam drove Sakura to the airport despite her protests the next day and asked her again to take someone along. Even if it weren't him, he would feel better knowing she had a protector. Of course, he understood that with the Keith women seducing the shifters, any man with enough training was nothing more than another set of eyes to watch over her. More often than not Sakura took down her quarries. Adam provided backup and partnership when there was more than one. They had come through many scrapes together, and he hated not being in Miami with her, but he would get there as soon as possible.

After she refused a protector, he comforted himself with knowing it was him or no one for Sakura, and he watched her leave. He checked his watch and dug into his jacket for his own boarding pass. He had a flight to Juneau to catch, and just the thought of meeting with shifters openly set his teeth on edge. Birk, the polar bear shifter, lover to Sakura's youngest sister, had agreed to talk to him after he explained what he needed, but he had no way of knowing if the man believed Adam was not setting a trap. On that same token, he didn't know if the shifter wanted revenge for what the Keiths had put him and his people through when they ran off with

Shiya. This meeting was a big risk on both sides, but Adam saw it as his only option.

A little over seven hours later, his flight touched down in Juneau, and Adam checked in to the villa he had arranged for. Once he'd refreshed himself with a shower and a change of clothes, he set out for his meeting. Being his first time in Juneau, he took in the small downtown area with shops, crowds of tourists walking along beside him, and at the end of the street a majestic mountain. He'd traveled to many countries with Sakura, and the world's natural beauty held the same appeal.

The saloon Birk had selected couldn't be missed on Franklin Street. He stepped into the establishment with his nerves stretched tight and tension stiffening the muscles across his back. Sawdust beneath his feet, he paused to take in his surroundings, realizing he had no idea what Birk looked like. The place was rustic in design, woodwork everywhere and a stuffed bear over the bar. He wondered what Birk and his people thought of that.

"Not one of mine," came a voice behind him. Adam spun to face the man who'd just passed through the doorway. He looked like a lumberjack in Adam's opinion, just as earthy as the establishment in a button up shirt, old jeans, and scuffed boots. Adam supposed with the overlong, dirty-blond hair, maybe a woman would find him appealing. For himself, he sensed a bit of danger lurking behind the friendly eyes and stayed on alert.

"Birk?" Adam asked to confirm.

"In the flesh." Birk moved past him without trying to shake his hand and led the way to an already occupied table. Adam frowned, but as they reached it, the two men sitting there stood, nodded a greeting to Birk, and then melted away. Were they the shifter's people or humans Birk had intimidated into doing his bidding? Birk sat down and gestured to the chair opposite him. "Have a seat."

Adam sat down. "How did you know it was me?"

Birk chuckled and tapped his nose. "You have a scent on you similar to Shiya's. I assume it's what her sister smells like."

Adam ground his teeth. He didn't like this shifter thinking about how Sakura smelled. He'd been intoxicated with her fresh, sweet scent for years, and loved it. Even without the nose of a bear, he recognized Sakura's unique fragrance, which was all her.

"Easy, partner," Birk teased. "I don't have designs on Sakura. Shiya is everything."

Adam's eyes widened. "That's an odd way of putting it."

"You would understand if you knew the bond we share."

"You and her?"

"My kind," Birk corrected. Birk paused as one of the men who'd been sitting at the table earlier returned with two beers. He set one in front of Adam. Birk nodded his thanks and drained half of his in one swallow. Adam took a cautionary sip and enjoyed the flavor. "Don't worry. It's not poisoned."

"How do you know I didn't come here to attack you?" Adam countered.

16

"You came alone."

Adam inferred a lot from the simple statement. Birk meant he was no match for Birk by himself, let alone the other shifters that might live in Juneau. He didn't bother asking how Birk knew he'd come alone. Adam had been taught how to know if he were being tracked, but apparently there was still a lot to learn. He had seen no one watching him, nor picked up on being followed to the villa or on the way to the bar. Then it occurred to him maybe Birk could smell him from the airport. Could he distinguish between all the humans that arrived in and left the city? If so, that blew his mind.

Birk chuckled and signaled to his friend for another beer. "Don't hurt your head over it."

Adam frowned. "You can't read minds."

"No, but I can tell you're trying to figure me out. Something you can use in your hunt, information to share with the Keiths?" This time, the amusement left the man's tone to be replaced with bitterness. "Tell me why you're here if it's not to try to kill me."

Adam glanced around, searching for Kotori, Shiya's other lover. "The other one isn't here? Or Shiya?"

Birk's blue eyes darkened. "Leave Shiya out of this."

Adam held up his hands. "That's exactly what I want. I don't want her to know about what we discuss, because..." He hesitated. "I don't want it to get back to the Keiths."

The shifter's eyes widened. "Now you have me intrigued."

Adam finished his beer and brushed a hand over his mouth. He rolled his shoulders and looked Birk in the eyes. "I want you to make me like you."

Birk's jaw dropped. His fresh glass of beer tumbled to the table and almost spilled, but he caught it in time. Some of the color in his cheeks vanished, but then his confusion turned to anger. "Why would you want that?"

Adam was prepared for the question. "The way I see it, the only way to get Sakura is to be a shifter." He paused and glanced around them. Birk waved away his concern that they would be overheard. No one seemed to pay them any mind, and he wondered how many of the patrons weren't human. Thinking that way made him fidget a bit in his seat. Now he wished he'd brought along a weapon as added protection. *No, I can't think that way anymore. They are no longer my enemy.*

Birk shook his head. "That makes no sense. From what I hear, Sakura hates my kind more than all the others, more so now with her sisters mated to shifters. The middle one is no longer human."

Adam puzzled over the word *mated*, but didn't question Birk about it. He'd learned about shifters finding partners they believed they were meant to be with and forming a bond that was unbreakable, but he knew the full meaning escaped humans.

Feeling self-conscious, he muttered, "Sakura loves me."

"So you want to control her. Is that it? Force her to be with you?"

"Of course not!" Adam half rose from his chair, but he remembered he was the one who needed Birk, and he reined in his temper. So far he had failed to convey how he felt because of his pride and because shifters tended to exude masculinity. He had no desire to look like a punk in front the man.

"Turning is dangerous. I'm sure you know you could die."

"*A mi plín.* I don't care. I'd risk anything to be with her. I know this is the best way."

"You love her," Birk said with dawning understanding. "I know about the Keiths. They are an arrogant family. They've been hunting my kind for generations, and they think somehow that makes them superior. The one thing they do respect is our strength and that we're not to be taken lightly. You believe by becoming what Sakura respects, she will look up to you."

"I don't wish to be above Sakura. I don't want to rule her. I want her to see me for more than the green man she once knew. As...what you are, she'll open her eyes. I know she will."

"And if she rejects you? Then what? In fact, you risk her deciding to kill the man she loves. That would hurt her a lot more, maybe even destroy her. Did you think of that?"

"Night and day," Adam said. "This isn't a decision I came to overnight. I know Sakura better than anyone. She's not the hard-hearted woman many make her out to be. She's strong physically, but emotionally, she can be very vulnerable. She's afraid to let me in, but it doesn't mean I haven't found a place already inside her. I will burrow deeper and deeper until she can't deny me."

"You could do that as a human."

He shook his head. "I never said I was perfect. I want her now. Besides, the biggest reason Sakura thinks she can't give in to her feelings is because she thinks she'll be much more open to the enemy's attack."

"If there is no longer a reason to fight…" Birk concluded, and Adam nodded.

Birk sat in silence for a while, having another beer. Adam nursed a second one but didn't drink much. He wanted all his faculties about him, and from the glance Birk gave him, he guessed the man knew his reservations. Here Adam was asking Birk to make him a shifter and yet, he couldn't trust them. Adam had no doubt that Birk felt the same. The man's next words confirmed it.

"I can't be sure this isn't some elaborate scheme. The Keiths will do anything to get their man. Granted, they usually use the beautiful Keith daughters to seduce the men, but since we are aware of who and what they are, maybe the family has come up with a new tactic."

Adam opened his mouth to respond, but Birk continued.

"That's why I'm meeting you and not Kotori. My friend believes this is a trap. I wanted to give you the benefit of the doubt. Kotori would just as soon rip off your head as talk to you."

Adam flinched at the image the words produced in his mind.

"We also agreed to keep Shiya out of the city for the time being."

Adam frowned. "You're holding her hostage?"

"Of course not! Shiya is our mate. As I said earlier, she's everything. We'll keep her safe no matter the threat."

"But she must want to see her family."

"She misses her sisters and her dad, but they're on different sides now. There's nothing any of us can do."

"I can make a difference," Adam insisted, leaning forward. "With Sakura. Give me the chance."

Birk studied his face for a long time, and Adam did his best to look trustworthy. He might have come in here not knowing what to expect, holding on to his own prejudices against shifters. Talking to Birk had felt awkward and even wrong at first. He'd always kept his distance, watching over Sakura while she seduced the men suspected of being something other than human. He'd hated seeing them touch her or her touching them, but he was never privy to conversation. He had been taught that shifters came off as human and could fool anyone who did not know to look for the signs. Adam found this to be untrue with Birk, unless the training referred to lower level shifters. Birk didn't give off any signs—no sudden shifting of the eyes, no violent temper, no claws forming from out of nowhere. Then again, Birk had no reason to lose control in this place. Juneau was his home, and clearly, he did not consider Adam a threat.

"If I'm changed," Adam said, "I am an immediate enemy to the Keiths. Correct?"

"Yeah."

"So, I'm not a part of any plot on their part."

"Good point." Birk slapped his hands down on the table. "Since neither I nor my friend can make shifters, it's out of our hands."

Disappointment tightened Adam's gut.

"But," Birk continued, "I might know someone. I'll explain everything. If this person is willing, you'll get what you want. If not, you will be killed."

Adam stared, looking for the joke. "You're serious."

"Deadly." He reached inside his jacket and felt around then pulled out a business card. Adam caught the word "antiques" on the front before Birk flipped the card over. He scribbled a name and number. "Give me a couple days."

Adam took the offered card and looked at the number. "Nine seven two. That's Texas, isn't it?"

Birk winked. "You don't mind traveling for what you want, do you?"

"Not at all." Adam stood and held out his hand. "*Gracias, amigo.*"

"No problem."

Adam left the saloon and walked along Marine Way. He had a lot to think about. The truth was, he had no way of knowing if Birk would tell his friend to kill him no questions asked. Birk had admitted himself his friend Kotori would just as soon end his life as look at him, especially if he thought Adam threatened Shiya's safety. The intensity in the man's words had shaken him. Adam believed these two creatures did love Shiya, and they wouldn't hesitate to attack anyone they thought would hurt her. He couldn't blame them for that. He would do the same for Sakura. In fact, he had done it on more than one occasion, but he'd done so in conjunction with his job.

When he reached his room after almost an hour and a half of walking around, he removed the card Birk had given him and read the name. *Laila Stark*. The person who could change Adam into a shifter was a woman, and only now as he lay back on his bed did he realize he'd neglected to ask what kind of animal she could make him, and what was the process—a bite? A scratch? He considered calling Birk but then decided to wait and see. He hated having to hold off two days because that left Sakura forty-eight hours without his protection. Too many out there gunned for the Keiths. Well, he would get there soon enough, and then they would talk. How he would break it to her, he had no idea, but he would.

After a few more moments of relaxation, Adam stood and moved to the desk to open his laptop. He had arrangements to make and a letter to write to Sakura just in case he died two days from now. He wanted her to understand how deeply he loved her and to be sure she never blamed herself. He doubted she would walk away from hunting shifters if one killed him, but she would at least be secure in what he had felt for her. He could offer nothing else but all of himself.

Chapter Three

Sakura wiped moisture from her forehead as she climbed into the rental and frowned at her surroundings. This was the fourth hotel she'd visited, yet none was the right place. Her feet hurt, her throat was dry, and her stomach growled because she'd neglected to eat breakfast. Why did it have to be so damn difficult to at least pin down the hotel? Then a new thought struck her. What if her mother hadn't died in a hotel but a motel, a cheaper establishment? She hated the thought considering she'd never stepped into anything below five star, but the beast that abducted her mother could have taken her to a seedy place where he'd be less likely to be found out.

She turned over the car's engine and made sure the A/C was on max and let the air cool her overheated body. Her sundress clung, and she fanned it, leaning close to the vent. While she hadn't really come to Florida to lie on the beach, the water and a mimosa called to her. Ever since she'd given her dad the excuse of a vacation, she wanted to stretch out and relax. Working nonstop got to a person after a while.

If Adam was here... She cut off such thoughts and drove the man from her mind. Adam declined coming along, and he didn't deserve her dwelling on thoughts of him. Let him rot in California! Of course, as much as she raged internally, she missed him. Her bed seemed bigger and lonelier at night, and for some stupid reason, she felt less safe.

"Okay, get a grip, Sakura. You've been taking care of yourself for years. You don't need a man to do it now."

After checking GPS on her phone, she found a likely strip of motels and decided to check them out. She jerked the car into gear and started off. Half hour later, she drew up to a building that screamed cheap. Sakura removed her sunglasses as she stepped out of the car and stared up at the building. Did someone really think they would class up this place by painting the doors and edging powder blue? Small potholes littered the parking lot, and the manicured bushes outside the main office seemed to be dying. Two giant palm trees leaned toward the lot, heavy with coconuts. Sakura peered back at the car as she approached the door. She'd probably be okay, but staying more than a minute to confirm whether this motel was the right one wasn't happening.

"Good morning," the chipper, blue-haired lady behind the counter greeted her. "Welcome to Miami. Will that be a room for one?"

"Thanks," Sakura said, deciding against admitting she wouldn't be staying. "I was wondering if any of your rooms have a view of this bridge." She'd made a copy of the picture and removed her mom from it to keep from scaring the people she questioned.

The old lady took the photocopy and squinted at it. "Oh, the Seven Mile Bridge. You know it's known all over the world. People come from everywhere to see it."

Sakura groaned. "Yes, but the view…"

"The view? Oh sure," the woman said in a conversational tone, "you can see the bridge from many motels. Not just this one. I—"

"I'm sorry," Sakura pushed between clenched teeth. "Perhaps I have the wrong motel."

Confusion colored the woman's face. "So, you don't want to stay in room twenty-four?"

Pain pulsed in Sakura's temple. "Room twenty-four?"

A toothy grin and a tap on the page. "Yes, this is room twenty-four. I know because I made that flamingo picture on the wall myself. I'm not so much into crafts lately since the arthritis has gotten so bad."

"Can I see the room?"

The woman blinked at Sakura's rudeness, but hope rose in her chest, and she found it hard to calm down. She might have actually found the place where her mother died. When the old woman grabbed a key from behind the counter, Sakura blew out a breath of relief. The progress out of the office and up the stairs at the end of the building seemed to take forever. At last they arrived outside the room, and Sakura again had to tamp down her impatience while the woman fumbled with the lock and key.

The door swung open, and Sakura stepped inside. Aqua colored walls, plastic stark white chairs sat around a small circle table, and full size bed crowded the tiny room. She spotted the flamingo picture right away and the view beyond it. Her heart hammered as she compared the view with the picture and found it a dead on match. On shaky legs, she crossed the threadbare carpet to the bed and stood beside it. An image of her mother lying there sprang to mind, and tears flooded her eyes. She clutched her stomach and rushed out of the room, gulping huge breaths of air.

"Are you okay, honey?"

Sakura gripped the railing outside on the landing and shut her eyes. Embarrassment at her weakness made her straighten despite the lightheadedness. All the old feelings came flooding back, of how helpless she'd felt when she found out her mother died. They hadn't been close. Sure, she'd loved her mother and thought she was the epitome of womanhood, but the two of them argued all the time. Her mother wanted her to depend a little more on the family, but Sakura continued to take the assignments that meant traveling the farthest away. She couldn't explain why she was always so cut off and so... The last time she had argued with her mother, the woman had accused her of being afraid of living. Sakura had been so offended, she refused to come home, even for meetings. Then her mother was gone, along with any opportunity to build a closer relationship.

"I'm fine," Sakura said, pulling her thoughts from the past. "Were you here five years ago?"

"Five years?" The old woman frowned. "Of course, honey. This is my business. If I'm not here, who will run it?"

Sakura pulled another picture from her purse, one of her mother when she lived. "Do you recognize this woman? Was she ever here?"

More squinting. "A lot of people come through here. I don't remember everybody." The old lady shook her head and handed back the picture. Sakura cursed silently. She was not an investigator. Her targets and all their information were emailed to her, and she read over the facts, deciding the best way to approach the shifter. Looking for clues to what happened to her mother seemed impossible. How did one get people to remember what they had forgotten? What questions were best to ask? She'd come all this way and even found the motel, but she had no idea of the next move. The room had obviously been cleaned and probably been used a dozen times or more by other guests.

"Thank you for your time," she said and started down the stairs. When she arrived at her own hotel, she sighed at the luxury, leather couches with accent pillows, beautiful paintings on the wall, lush carpet on the floor, fresh flowers on the table, and best of all a muted color scheme that was both relaxing and classy.

She walked to the bed with its turned back coverlet and mint on the pillow and flopped down, groaning. A ding on her cell phone brought her head up, and she checked the display, annoyed that she hoped it was Adam texting. Instead, a number she didn't recognize flashed on the screen. She read the message.

"Hi, Sakura. It's Roger Port. Care to have drink with me?"

She frowned and texted back. *"As if your name should mean something to me?"*

"Lol. Beautiful ladies should not be cruel to us lesser creatures. You can say I'm tech support."

Then she recalled the name. Her dad had hired Roger to replace her sister Shiya in gathering info on shifters. Now that Shiya was no longer their computer person since she had run off with a couple of polar bear shifters, they needed someone with her skill set. She hadn't had the chance to meet Roger face to face before she left San Diego.

"Sorry, Roger. I'm not in town at the moment."

"I know. You're in Miami. So am I. So how about that drink?"

Irritation rose, and she pressed her lips together. Had her dad sent Roger because she refused to take along a protector? No, if he had, it wouldn't be this guy. They had plenty of strong, capable men in their employ that could do the job. A computer nerd was the last person he would send. Then she considered whether Roger could give her clues on how to find information on her mother's death. She had no intention of sharing what she was doing because he might report back to her dad, but maybe he could help without realizing.

She let him know she'd be happy to meet him that evening for a drink and spent the rest of the day doing just what she had been wanting to, sunning beside the pool in a bikini and drinking a mimosa. When it was time to get ready, she returned to her room, showered, and chose a deep purple asymmetrical dress with one shoulder and an open back. An opaque strip of cloth slanted across her breasts, her waist, and her hips, connected by sheer strips at the upper part of her belly, a bit of her hip and across her thighs, making it appear she showed a lot more skin. She loved the dress because of how it fit her form like a glove and made her feel sexy. Four-inch heels completed her ensemble, and she brushed her hair until it shined and hung in a straight sheet several inches below her shoulders. In her experience, men liked long hair, so she kept it that way, especially since her job entailed seducing said men.

Ready, she left her room and accepted the hotel's complimentary ride to the lounge where Roger agreed to meet. She strode through the entrance and allowed her eyes to adjust to the dim lighting. A red lit ceiling illuminated the oddly shaped bar in the center of the room, lined with chair stools. Along the sides of the room were tall tables and chairs, where patrons enjoyed their drinks and food. Sakura scanned the faces at the bar and at the tables for anyone who might be her date. The bartender, wiping a glass dry with a towel, caught her gaze and winked. She resisted rolling her eyes and continued her search.

At a table near the back, a man in black slacks and crisp white shirt stood up from his table. He straightened stylish glasses and then brushed overlong, dark hair from his forehead. *Not exactly the nerdy look*, she thought, acknowledging his wave. Sakura walked over to him, noting if she removed her heels, they might be the same height.

"Roger?"

"The one and only." He held out his hand. "And you're Sakura. I've seen pictures of you. Wow, they don't do you justice. You're beautiful."

She lowered her gaze and thanked him, then caught herself. The coy, sweet thing was a persona she used for work when the guy was the type to like it. She had no need to be anything but herself with Roger.

"Thanks, but don't feel like you have to kiss up to the boss's daughter."

He grinned and held her chair while she sat down. "You don't think you're beautiful?"

She shrugged. If she said she did, she'd come off vain. If she denied it, he would probably shower more compliments on her. "So what are you doing in Miami? Are you checking up on me?"

"Yes."

She blinked at him, and he chuckled.

"I don't have to work in an office, you know. I can do what I do anywhere. Since I got the systems up and running, I thought I'd take a few days for myself."

"That's the running excuse," she muttered.

He didn't seem to have heard her. "My report on you says you travel a lot more than you're home. In fact, it was rare for you to be in San Diego, and I'd missed you by a few hours."

Sakura had no problem with the fact that he had a report on her. All of the field staff had dossiers. The hunters didn't just study their prey. They figured out the best person to send for the job and what skills would match best. Now that they were down to just Sakura, she didn't figure they had much of a choice as far as the women."

"I met everyone else," Roger was saying. "I wanted to get to know you in person, especially if I'm going to recommend other women."

Sakura gasped. "Other women? My dad intends to hire women to replace my sisters? He never told me that!"

"He didn't say so, but you can't do it alone, right?"

For some reason his words seemed to hold a challenge, but she refused to rise to it. "Makes sense, I guess."

He nodded. "But first you. Tell me what you'd like to drink. I'll do all in my power to please you."

"Sit still," Sakura told him and rose. "I'll get us something." Her habit was never to allow a man to have access to her drink, and she didn't care if Roger did work for her father. A cautious nature would not be denied. She procured a beer for him and a mojito for herself, including Bacardi, lime, mint syrup, and club soda. She also asked for a double order of fries because she hadn't eaten much that day, and she was starving. Having more alcohol on an empty stomach might spell trouble, so she wanted to head it off.

"Thanks." Roger took the offered beer and snagged a French fry. Sakura ate a few and sipped her drink. Roger leaned toward her as if to keep others from overhearing, but she doubted with the music vibrating the air around them anyone could listen in. "So why are you in Miami? This doesn't seem like your scene."

"And you would know my scene?" she countered.

He studied her face. "Somewhere exotic maybe. With an ocean between you and home."

She glared.

He held up hands, grinning. "I'm not judging you. Who knows, I might feel the same. I travel all over myself, but I'm new to Cali. So far, I like what I see."

Sakura knew he aimed the statement at her. Roger worked hard to get close to her, which was hardly necessary. From the way his gaze dropped every so often to her legs, exposed beneath her dress, she assumed he would have no problem should she ask him to join her in her room later. For a while now, Adam had been her only lover, and she usually kept at least two. None lasted more than a year, except Adam. *Okay, stop thinking of him, damn it!* Maybe she should invite Roger to her room. If she took on a new lover, it might help dissipate the feelings she had built for Adam.

"Thanks," she said in a deep, sultry voice, and she tilted her head to the side while studying him. Color rose in his cheeks. She crossed one leg over the other at the side of the tiny table and made sure to bump his leg. "Oh, sorry."

He shifted in his chair. "No worries."

"So I guess you're a genius, huh? The way you recovered our system in no time?"

He preened. "Me? No, just know a little about computer systems. Your sister was pretty good in the way she wiped out most of the data, but she outsmarted herself in the end. There was another backup—granted in pieces of code. I simply rooted around in it and solved the puzzle. Viola."

"Oh, viola," she said, amused. "I don't know computers, but I'm guessing the rooting around took hours."

"Hours, days, weeks. I have no social life."

"I don't believe you." She bumped him again, this time letting him know it was on purpose. "You look like you know how to have fun."

The man practically panted.

She waggled a finger at him. "I bet you are so smart, you could find anyone, anywhere. Not just shifters either. Wait, you're probably like those guys...um..."

His brows rose. "Those guys?"

"The ones on that show. They pick up clues from crime scenes." She felt like an idiot. The stretch from computer wiz to a CSI investigator was so wide, but she hadn't been able to come up with any other way to lead the conversation where she wanted.

Roger nodded. "Ah, yes, *that* show. I'm a strong guy, but I think a crime scene with all its blood would be beyond me."

Sakura almost slumped with disappointment.

"But once it was on a computer, I could go through it easy enough. Hell, I could probably even hack into the medical examiner's office computer if I wanted."

Medical Examiner. His words triggered an idea in Sakura. Why hadn't she thought of it before? Someone must have found her mother's body and called the police and the medical examiner. Her family had many contacts in official capacities, and they had covered up more than one incident that involved shifters to keep the general public in the dark. She couldn't outright use one of the contacts to gain information because it might get back to her dad, but maybe if she had the excuse of another case, she could get into the office.

She looked at Roger and considered asking him to prove his ability to do a little hacking, but decided against it. Although unlikely, he still might be a spy for her dad to see what she was up to. Better to forge a way with the Keith name on the pretext of a case. Then she could play everything by ear when she reached the medical examiner's office.

Sakura and Roger chatted some more about inconsequential things, and then he saw her back to her hotel. Outside her room, she turned to him to bid him good night. He stilled and looked at her door.

"Is something wrong, Roger?" she asked.

He offered a sheepish grin. "I thought you might invite me in."

She put a hand on her hip. "Is it in my report that I jump into bed with men I've just met?"

"No, no, I'm sorry. I didn't mean to offend you."

She smirked. "You didn't." Leaning forward, she kissed his cheek and smelled his cologne, a nice manly scent that awakened her libido but didn't quell thoughts of how she wished that damn Adam were in Miami. Before she could use Roger to get rid of the desire, she slipped the key card into the slot and entered her room.

The lights were off even though she remembered leaving one on. She frowned and crossed the room, trying to remember where the switch was. Rolling her eyes, she turned to retrace her steps, and a hand snaked out of the darkness to encircle her waist. She opened her mouth, but another hand clamped across her lips. Sakura didn't hesitate to bring the heel of her shoe down on the attacker's foot. He howled in pain, and she kicked backward, her foot glancing off the side of his leg. If she'd aimed better, she'd have taken out his knee.

"Son of a—" the man growled.

Sakura didn't allow him to finish the curse. She

thrust her head back and cracked him in the chin. He hit the floor hard. She scrambled away and fumbled for the light. A lamp came on and illuminated the room. The man on the floor rolled to his hands and knees and jumped up.

"You're not going anywhere," she snapped and ran after him. He moved with a speed too fast for a human. Sakura jerked her dress up and unsheathed the knife on her upper thigh. She hit the balcony door seconds after the man did, but when she stepped out onto the platform, empty hot air met her. To the left stretched an unbroken line of balconies across the building. To the right were more of the same. She ran to the railing and peered over the side then gasped. Like a monkey, the man leaped from one balcony to the next, descending in a zigzag pattern until he disappeared into the open doors of one room. Were there monkey shifters, or was this agility common to his kind, whatever that was?

She didn't bother going down to the lower floor to see if she could find him. He would be long gone, and since he obviously had business with her, she didn't doubt he would show up again. Besides, she had seen his face. If she ran across him, the outcome of their fight would be very different.

Chapter Four

Sakura spent the next few days allowing Roger to take her out dancing and exploring Miami. She dragged him along shopping so she could pick his brain a little more. Surprised she could wrangle so much info from the man, she reminded herself to have her dad lecture him about being so open. For now, his loose lips were a big help. She found out he had set up logons for all of the field staff, and she could sign in to the database at any time to gain information about shifters. She no longer had to rely on waiting for an email or making a call to headquarters. The system was not complete yet, but eventually, Roger informed her, she would be able to pick up an assignment at any time, enter new information she had learned, search for contacts, and even make appointments with said contacts.

"In fact," he bragged, "I'll make it so you can log in from your phone and find someone to help you in any capacity, wherever you are in the world. Specialties will be listed like fighting style, computer hacking, financial, government connections—you name it. And there will be clearance levels, of which yours will go to the top."

She smiled at him. "I feel so special."

"You should." He reached a hand out to touch her hair, and she let him for the moment. "You're very special, Sakura."

"You've said that or something close to it every time we go out. I'm beginning to think you're not sincere."

His eyes widened. "I am, but I have to keep trying, don't I? I want to get close to you." He touched her hand, and Sakura heard cars honking their horns behind them. She remained where she was, knowing the light had changed and not caring. Roger had been content to let her drive, and not for the first time she wondered how much he would let her lead. What about in the bedroom, should they take it there?

"I'll keep that in mind," she told him, and drove on. They hit South Beach and visited Lincoln Road Mall. Crowds of tourists walked along, exploring the shops and the street vendors. Sakura found a few vintage outfits and unique jewelry that would go well with dresses she already owned. Roger insisted on playing the gentleman by holding her bags, and she didn't argue with him.

While Roger haggled over some bauble a vendor sold, she wandered on. She stood on tiptoe, squinting behind her sunglasses and then lowered them to study a man not far away. No doubt about it, the sandy blond head, slim shoulders, and smooth gait belonged to her attacker. She glanced over her shoulder at Roger and then weaved her way through the crowd. Her date would have to catch up with her later. For now, work called, and she wasn't letting the bastard get away.

When the man stepped out from the pedestrian only area into the cross street at Lenox Avenue, he picked up speed, and Sakura followed. She touched a hand to the knife on her outer thigh and took mental inventory of the various other weapons on her person, glad she'd worn flat, comfortable shoes. On the opposite side of Lenox, they continued walking and then reached a parking garage. The man disappeared into it. Sakura looked around and hurried after him. Somewhere, someone slammed a car door, but she didn't spot the person. No one stood nearby, and as she looked up and down the line of parked vehicles, she couldn't spot the shifter.

"Damn," she whispered. "He is not giving me the slip again." She ran down the nearest row of cars, and out popped her attacker, an arm extended as if he intended to clothesline her. Sakura bobbed low and brought her fist up to punch him in the side. The man slammed against a car.

"You bitch," he growled.

For the insult, she punched him in the mouth and then bounced back on her toes, fists raised. "That's for breaking into my room. Now, you want to tell me why you came after me?"

"You're going to pay for that with your life," he threatened, and his eyes changed in an instant, going from blue irises with white on either side to amber ones, surrounding elliptical pupils and no white at all. He curved his hands in front of him almost as if he begged like a puppy, but short fingernails grew out to blackened claws.

Sakura fell back a step. There was no doubt in her mind now that she dealt with a shape-shifter. "What are you?"

He advanced on her. "I'm the man who will take down Sakura Keith."

So he did know who she was. Not that she'd doubted it. The family name, more than the faces, were known all over the world. Shifters and a few select humans who knew how to keep their mouths shut were privy to what her family did. Often Sakura could slip into the shifter's world under an assumed name and take down the enemy long before he identified her. As a normal precaution, she had checked into the Miami hotel with false identification, and yet, she'd been found out.

"Since it seems we're making corny declarations," she said as she raised the hemline of her dress and pulled out her knife, and then checked that they were alone. "I'm going to gut you and send you back to wherever you came from."

"We'll see about that."

He lunged at her, and she easily parried his swing. One thing she'd been taught from the beginning and that was to avoid being bitten or scratched by a shifter. Some, but not all, could make others like them with one of those methods. Not knowing if this thing had that ability, she took no chances. She would have to make sure he didn't land any blows.

They performed a deadly dance, the man leaping at her, and Sakura bobbing out of the way in time. She tried slicing into his belly, but he was fast. Looking into his menacing eyes told her the problem was much more than his speed though. He had something more going for him, and she needed to be extra careful. At times like this, she realized why she needed a protector.

The man feigned left, and Sakura tried moving with him. The next second he brought a long, thin arm down over her head. As if in slow motion, she saw the claws and knew they'd drag along her face. Her heart thundered, deafening her. She bent backward, balancing momentarily on the balls of her feet. Her thighs burned, and back muscles cramped. She swung up to block the blow. Shirt material ripped, and she hit the ground. Another slice through the air, and she dragged her knife across his arm. The man howled in pain and drew back. He banged against a car, holding his forearm as blood gushed between his fingers. Sakura rolled over and regained her footing. She checked her blouse. The material hung in ribbons, exposing her bra, but her skin remained unscathed. She breathed a sigh of relief.

The two of them circled each other, Sakura not daring to take her eyes off the man. He bared his teeth, hissing and growling. She assumed he meant the tactic to scare her, and it did a little. Fear always drove her adrenaline higher and made her stronger and faster, so she welcomed it. She spun the knife in her hand and flexed her shoulders. *Time to end this before someone catches us.*

Sakura raised her knife, her muscles tight and ready. The man cracked his knuckles with each curl of his fingers. If possible, the claws seemed more menacing, but she forced her attention away from them to watch his eyes. Where they went, that's where the man would go.

She decided if she was to overcome his speed, she'd win this fight, and that meant striking first with intent to kill.

Swallowing all fear and hesitation, she charged.

"Sakura, no!"

The weight hit her hard in the back, sending her flying forward, and because she'd been going that way anyway, she couldn't stop or control how she smashed into the shifter. The slight barrier pushed against the tip of her knife and then gave, allowing the weapon to sink deep into flesh. Sakura, the man, and the bastard on her back hit one of the parked cars and then dropped to the ground. Thinking of the shifter's claws, Sakura didn't have time to lie there, wondering what happened. She thrust out from the sandwich of men, pulling her knife with her and rolled over onto her back. Roger stumbled to his knees and leaned over her. She aimed the now bloodied knife at him.

"You'd better explain yourself right now," she panted.

Roger's eyes were wide, and he'd gone pale. He held up his hands in surrender then struggled to his feet and backed away. "I...he had claws. He was about to kill you."

Sakura glanced at the shifter who lay still on the ground. By sheer luck, her knife entered his heart. She blew out a breath and stood up. "You idiot. Stay behind the computer where you belong. You almost got me killed."

"I was just—"

She glared at him, and he fell silent. "You were trying to be my hero. I have people who are trained to fight alongside me, and they don't put my life at risk." His head hung, and she groaned under her breath. "Thanks for trying. I appreciate it."

"Yeah, right." He chuckled.

Sakura pulled her cell phone out and hesitated. She eyed Roger. "You can help me a lot more if you've got a contact here, someone I can call for cleanup?"

A slow smile spread over Roger's face. "Of course." He pulled out his cell as well, but Sakura stopped him from making the call. She peered over his shoulder and recorded the number to her own phone.

"Try to keep anyone from seeing, okay?"

Roger nodded as she strode some ways from him back to the street. Cars zoomed by. A man sipped from a Styrofoam cup while he drove his scooter. She noticed how he looked at her rather than the parked delivery truck ahead of him and gave him a pointed stare. He turned away and yelped when he almost ran up onto the lowered ramp. She shook her head.

On the opposite side of the street stood an old Spanish style building, its courtyard a jungle of overgrown bushes and palm trees. She checked the windows above and considered whether anyone might have seen the fight in the parking garage, but doubted it. After confirming no one walked nearby, she dialed the number Roger gave her.

The contact picked up on the second ring. "Is this Charles Aiza?"

"Yes," he said with hesitation in his tone. She guessed he saw the six one nine area code and knew it must be someone from her family.

"I need a cleanup," she told him, without identifying herself first. "Can you handle it for me?"

"O-of course. Yes, I can. Um, Ms. Keith?"

So he knew who she was, and they were on the same page. Good. "Please refrain from using that name." Were they all newbies now?

"I'm sorry. Of course."

Not long after, men arrived at their location. They were nondescript, drove a plain white van, and said nothing as they scooped up the dead shifter, searched the area for anything that might have been left behind, and were gone.

"Wow, first time I've seen that," Roger said behind her.

Sakura shrugged. "I have, all over the world, and even with varied languages spoken, it's the same. They come in, do their job, and melt away. I always wonder who they are in their regular life. Do they have kids? Do they go bowling with the boys on Thursday nights?"

Roger grinned, and his manner was lighthearted, but from his color, and the way he clenched his hands into fists in his pockets, Sakura guessed the murder got to him. A computer nerd would not face this kind of danger, and she knew firsthand how it could get to be too much, even with experience. That's why she humanized the pickup crew talking about their home life, her way of dealing with what she'd just done.

Sakura turned to face him and pulled his hand from his pocket. She slipped her fingers through his and pressed close. "Hey."

Energy seemed to vibrate from the man, and she was struck again how cute he was for a desk jockey.

"Let's forget work for a while and have some fun."

His eyebrows rose. "I thought that's what we were doing all this time."

She laughed. "That was daytime fun. Let's go dancing. I haven't shaken my thing in a while."

"Your thing?"

"Yes, my thing. Are you up for it, or do I need to find another date?"

"Oh I'm up, *very* up."

Sakura rolled her eyes, and they took the long walk back to where he had parked the car. She returned to her room long enough to shower and change into something sexy, and then she and Roger hit Miami hard. Collins Avenue provided them with a nightclub that made Sakura feel like they were in Las Vegas rather than Miami. Flashing colored lights, multi-colored couches, and crazy entertainment amid loud, vibrating music. While Sakura danced to the beat, Roger tapped her on the shoulder, and she glanced over to him. He pointed with his chin to the six-foot-four blond man on the upper level, surrounded by a few too attentive men and a couple of half-naked beauties. Sakura's eyes widened.

"Is that—?"

"Yeah," Roger yelled above the noise. "They get celebrities in here all the time."

"Nice." She grinned and considered going up to meet the delicious specimen of manhood, but thought better of it. He looked like he'd come out to have some fun like the rest of them, and he didn't need some fan girl hanging onto him. While she raised her glass to sip her drink, the man caught her gaze, and the most perfect lips formed a smile. He raised his own glass in a silent toast, and Sakura's heartbeat went erratic. *Damn, Miami's all right!*

She and Roger danced most of the night away, but when she'd removed her heels and her feet still hurt, she decided to call it a night. They pushed their way through the thinning but still thick crowd and worked to get to the exit. Just when Sakura reached the door, a man pressed a napkin into her hand. She blinked at him and looked down at it. A number was scrawled in sloppy script in the center along with a name.

"He says give him a call," the man said, and Sakura lost her breath. She nodded, and the man faded back into the crowd. Yeah, like she was going to make a big time celebrity her lover. Sure, it would be hot as hell, but it was also the fastest way to get her face in the media, a sure method to kill the false identity deal. The experience might make a good story to share with her sisters though. Then she remembered she'd been cut off from her sisters, maybe forever. She sighed and left the nightclub to return to her hotel.

"You really know how to have fun," Roger said outside her room. He stumbled against her, but she brought her hands up to keep him from sending them both to the floor.

"You've had too much to drink, sir."

"I'd like to have a different drink."

She wrinkled her nose, laughing. "Wow, you get cornier when you're drunk."

"I'm not drunk." He proved he was by swaying, and she pushed him against the door to hold him up. He sighed, staring into her eyes. "I've never made love to a black woman before."

"And you're under the assumption you will tonight?"

"I am always hopeful."

She let her gaze travel his form, from head to toe. "You're not too bad to look at," she teased and ran a finger over his chest to his abs. She wasn't surprised to find the latter nice and firm.

"I've got a lot more you haven't seen."

"Oh really?" She leaned in even closer, and their mouths needed just a nudge to touch. He played the game with her, not closing the space, allowing them both to be tantalized but not yet giving in. "What are we talking?"

Roger smirked. "Why don't you find out for yourself?"

"You're a very dirty man, Roger Port."

"Get dirty with me, Sakura Keith."

She made a purring sound, considering it. The next instant, she found herself on the other side of the hall, having bumped her head against it, and Adam with his back to her and hand wrapped around Roger's neck, raising him up off his feet.

"*Quien carajo eres tú?*" Adam roared. "You don't touch her!"

Sakura blinked. "Adam!"

Her lover ignored her and threw Roger down on the floor as if he weighed nothing. Roger scrambled backward on his hands and ass, but Adam stalked over to him. Adam hit him, and blood spattered Roger's shirt and Adam's, pouring from Roger's nose. Sakura ran over and grabbed Adam's arm. He shook her off. Another punch to Roger's ribs, but Roger managed to somewhat block the hit. If he didn't, Sakura was pretty sure he would have had broken ribs.

"Stop," she shouted. "Adam, leave him alone. You have no right to do this."

Roger somehow managed to twist away from Adam's hold and got to his feet. He took a fighting stance Sakura might be proud of, if his nose weren't obviously broken. His gaze narrowed, he waited for Adam to try hitting him again, but she darted between the two men, facing Adam.

"I said stop. You don't get to decide who I'm with, Adam. I made that clear the day we started seeing each other. I told you an open relationship or nothing. You agreed. So don't come here acting like you own me."

Adam sneered, and she could have sworn something shifted in his eyes. "That gives you the right to be *una puta?*"

"You did not call me a whore!" She punched him in the stomach as hard as she could, and she could do damage to most men. Even Adam had pissed her off in the past, and she'd let him have it. He'd winced and said she hit like a man. She had taken it as a compliment and told him not to play with her. Tonight though, maybe it was all the alcohol she had consumed, but punching Adam was almost like punching a brick wall. She cried out in pain and doubled over, holding her hand. All the drink she took in over the last few hours threatened to come shooting out of her mouth.

"Baby, your hand." He whisked her into his arms.

"You shouldn't have done that. Are you okay?"

"No, I'm not," she breathed between clenched teeth. She had no strength to push him away when he dug through her purse and found her key card. He used it to open her bedroom door, glared at Roger, and then shut the door in his face.

Adam rushed her to a chair and knelt in front of her to examine her hand. She tried to pull away, but he wouldn't let go, gingerly checking each finger to be sure she could move them. Sakura winced, but it was clear she hadn't broken any bones.

He let her hand go with apparent reluctance and stood.

"What are you doing here, Adam? You said you weren't coming."

"I finished up a little business and thought I'd join you." He glared down at her. "You said you were coming to investigate your mom's death, not pick up new lovers."

"I'm grown, and I can do whatever the hell I want to. I certainly don't need to answer to you." She stood, hating for the moment how small he made her feel. He towered above her anyway, which pissed her off even more. "You never fought my former lovers. I kept you around because it didn't bother you if I enjoyed other men. Now you're acting like this."

"You *kept* me around?" He took a step toward her, and she found herself stumbling back. Adam was always self-possessed and strong, but he displayed a level of aggression she had never seen in him. She didn't think he'd hurt her, but the way he behaved confused her.

Anger sparked in his eyes, making them appear almost black. He reached out and raised her chin, the grip tight, but not painful. "I'm here because you want me. You can't help yourself."

Her mouth fell open. "Oh, really?"

"Yes, really." He dropped a hand to the front of her dress and circled a breast without touching the tip. "When I am not around you are...*bellaco*. Only I can satisfy you."

Sakura recognized the slang word for horny, not a literal translation. She learned a lot from him over the years—too much—and she was still angry with him over his attitude. Never mind that his closeness actually ignited the horniness he accused her of feeling when he was gone. She realized for all the teasing she'd engaged in with Roger, she didn't feel a fraction with him of what she felt now in Adam's presence. Looking into her lover's eyes, she deduced Adam knew it, too.

"You're getting a little above yourself, aren't you?"

She said the wrong thing. Adam grabbed her around the waist and backed her up until she hit the wall. His narrowed gaze raked her from head to toe, and when he curled fingers in the front of her dress, she opened her mouth to protest, but it was too late. He ripped the material straight down to her navel. The dress fell from her shoulders to her hips and pooled on the floor.

"Adam!"

His eyes widened, as if his actions surprised him. He took a step back and ran fingers through his hair, an expression of confusion on his face. "I don't..."

"Adam, what's going on with you? You're not like

your usual self." She touched his arm as he turned away, and he flinched.

"Don't touch me, Sakura."

She gasped, hurt tightening her chest. Maybe she had no right to be hurt, especially since it was obvious he didn't feel the same as he did in the past, wasn't as accepting of her lifestyle. "If you don't want to be here, then get out."

"Not wanting you isn't the problem! Look at you, Sakura."

She looked down at herself. Since a bra would have shown above the skimpy dress, she hadn't worn one, but she found no reason to hide her breasts now that Adam had exposed them. She stood there in bikini panties and nothing else.

"I want to eat you," he snapped. "Every bit of you, from your toes to your pussy to your lips."

"I've never turned you away from my bed, Adam." She put a hand on her hip, and even though you made me mad, I'm not now. We've argued like cats and dogs because makeup sex is hot."

"If I take you like this, I don't know what will happen."

She frowned. "Like what? You look good to me."

He did, too. His black hair tussled about his head, a new wild, almost dangerous look, in his eyes. Even his muscles seemed more defined, and Adam already had a body every man could envy. He gave off an aura of power she'd never known before from him, and she liked it. The man didn't understand how he turned her on right then.

He had been glancing toward the balcony as she examined him, but the minute she thought of how much he excited her, he breathed in deep and turned an intense gaze on her. "Sakura."

"What?"

He took a step toward her, and she tried backing up, but the wall kept her where she stood. "You're turned on," he said, his tone an accusation.

"So?" She raised her eyebrows in challenge.

A large hand flattened on the wall beside her head and another on the opposite side. "I can't leave."

"Who's asking you to?"

"It's not..." He shut his eyes, but he breathed deep again, and the moan he gave off was almost feral. Goose bumps broke out on her arms, and she practically purred in response. Without opening his eyes, Adam placed a hand over her mouth and shook his head. "Don't."

She pulled his hand down. "Aw, come on, Adam. I like this game. You look like you're about to lose control, and here I am a helpless maiden waiting to be ravaged by the big bad—"

"Stop!" he insisted.

She fell silent.

His hands moved from the wall to rove her hips, the outsides of her thighs, and around to her ass. He gave the cheeks a squeeze, a little too roughly. She bit her lip.

"Adam, why don't you open your eyes?"

He didn't answer but raised her chin and covered her mouth with his. The invasion of his tongue between her lips wasn't a request, but a demand. He swept the warm interior, taking what he wanted and left Sakura trembling. She curled her fingers into his shirt and pulled him closer. She stretched up to her toes and arched into his chest, hungry for more, but Adam pushed her back until she bumped the wall. He followed with his hard body, pressing her tight, exploring her mouth while his hands skimmed over her form. He found the line of her panties and ripped them off, then tossed the ragged material away. His thick fingers parted her folds and sank into her wetness. She whimpered, gasping against his mouth. He pumped his digits deep inside her until the heel of his palm thumped her swollen clit. The movement skyrocketed her toward an orgasm, but Adam wasn't satisfied. Even as he kept kissing her, he tore out of his clothes and kicked his shoes off. When he was naked, he grabbed her around the waist and hoisted her off her feet. Sakura scarcely had time to realize what he intended before he plunged his cock into her pussy. Her butt hit the wall, but he plowed hard, grinding his shaft home. She lost all strength, shocked at his size. Seemingly overnight, his cock had grown, so big it stretched her walls, and a tiny sliver of pain made her clutch his shoulders and turn her head so she could speak.

"Adam," she managed to whisper, "you're so thick. I'm not sure…"

"Don't tell me no, Sakura." He moved from his lips to her throat, and not once did he slow his thrusts. *"Por favor."*

She hesitated, partly scared at this wildness she hadn't seen before and somewhat excited, too. What he did to her body felt good, but it also seemed like his control was slipping. She had a choice to give in to her nerves or enjoy the pleasure he offered.

"Don't stop, baby," she murmured, and he pumped so hard, banging the wall, she wondered if any second the plaster would give. While his roughness hurt it felt incredible, too, better than she remembered sex with Adam had ever felt—and making love with him had always been explosive.

He raised her legs and wrapped them around his waist, then held her ass. Sakura's breast flattened against his chest, the little silky hairs tickling her stiff peaks. She held onto him, but it hardly seemed necessary. His pecs flexed, but it didn't seem like he had to struggle at all with her weight.

She shut her eyes and found the pulse at his throat, nipping it. Adam made an odd sound and raised her head. He claimed her mouth again, slanting his over hers and kissed her brutally. While he pinned her in place, her orgasm slammed through her system, and she screamed in his mouth. He pulled out and carried her to the table.

"The bed's right—" she began.

He dropped her on the end and plowed inside her heat. Sakura fell back, but before she hit the table, Adam had brushed everything off it. He crushed her on the unyielding surface, holding the opposite end with both hands and driving deep into her pussy. Sakura opened her mouth to moan, but no sound came out. She tried winding her arms around Adam's neck, but she could do no more than lie beneath him, letting him have his way. Her core muscles began to twine for another orgasm, but he withdrew.

"Adam."

This time he looked at her, his eyes open. They appeared feverish to her, so dark. She had no time to question him or look deeper before he flipped her onto her belly so that her legs hung over the side of the table. He lined his body with hers, and she reached back quickly to cover her butt.

"I know we do it back there sometimes, but there's no way you're fitting that monster in me tonight."

She glanced at him over her shoulder, and he blinked then straightened. "*Lo siento*. I was too rough." He took a step back, but Sakura grabbed his hand. She went up to her toes and arched her back, pushing her butt in the air. A little wiggle in invitation had Adam staring, hunger in his gaze. He hadn't come yet, and she'd never let him go unsatisfied.

"I was ready to come again. You're going to let me go like this?" she teased.

His chest rose and fell again, as if he breathed in her scent. "I can't."

"Nope, you can't," she agreed, grinning. Her pussy was worn out and starting to get sore, but she didn't care. Glancing down, she took in his cock. Definitely, way bigger than it was the last time they'd shared a bed. Hell, if it were possible in the two days since she'd seen him, she would have thought the man got some kind of procedure, but Adam had never needed to be ashamed of his equipment, and he knew how to use it. "Come on, baby. I'm still wet."

Adam lowered his eyelids so she couldn't see his eyes. He clamped his jaw down, and when he touched her hips, she felt like he struggled with something. He stepped closer to her. The tip of his thick cock brushed her butt cheek. She shut her eyes. *If this crazy man tries to get that thing in my butt, I will kill him.*

Despite the butterflies in her belly, she couldn't wait until he filled her. The way he stretched her was like being a virgin again, fresh and new, being schooled by her lover. She waited. Adam ran his shaft head over her cheeks. He replaced his member with fingers that pressed to her back entrance.

An angry growl pierced the air, and he plunged into her sex, deep and hard. She yelped at the sudden entry. Adam dragged her back a bit from the table, large hands engulfing her waist. He thumped hard, driving her forward. Just before her pelvis hit the table, his fingers were there, blocking the way, but that didn't stop him from leaning over her body and grinding hard into her pussy. She lay on the surface, her breasts flattened under her. Adam pulled her back and drove in at incredible speed. Her mind spun, the sensations overwhelming. She whimpered his name, and his answer was a grunt. He didn't stop pumping into her until she had come a second time. When she cried out, gasping and shaking, he raised her hips, pinched her clit, and stilled. The next instant, his hot seed flooded her pussy.

Sakura's knees gave out, and Adam pulled back. He raised her in his arms and carried her to the bed. When he dropped her onto the mattress, she looked up at him, but he'd already turned away. The room plunged into darkness, and shortly after, the mattress sank under his weight. She licked her lips.

"Adam?"

He didn't answer. In the darkness, he fingered her pussy, and she winced. He pulled back and reached for her hand. Not even a fumble, she thought though the blinds were closed, and her eyes had yet to adjust to the lack of light. He guided her hand to his cock, and she was surprised to find it stiff. Damn, spend two days away from the man, and his libido shoots through the roof.

She wrapped her fingers around the shaft and began stroking slow and easy. Adam snaked an arm out and dragged her closer to him. A shudder passed over his big form as he lay in silence. "If you want, I can suck it."

She didn't like tasting her own essence, which was why Adam never kissed her after he'd gone down on her. She had always liked that in him. Previous lovers tried to kiss her afterward as if they wanted to punish her for them having done it. None of them had lasted long.

When Adam still didn't speak, she started to move so she could suck his cock, but his hold tightened. He had no intention of letting her go. She lay in his arms, stroking him, and after a long while, he came a second time, his come squirting into her hand and onto her belly. He let her go so she could get cleaned up, but by the time she returned from the bathroom, the man was ready again.

"A little rest," she said, and he turned her over so she lay facedown on the bed. He climbed behind her, lining her body with his own. She felt his cock, tight and thick on her ass. His hands covered hers and then slid to her wrists. Nervous energy pulsed through her body, and she caught her bottom lip between her teeth.

"Por favor," he whispered, his voice ragged. She understood then. Adam hadn't spoken earlier because he couldn't. Desire took such sharp hold of him, he'd been unable to do anything other than ravage her body.

"Yes."

He entered her once again from behind and didn't stop until she collapsed from exhaustion.

Chapter Five

Sakura woke up to light pushing its way around the sides of the blinds, enough so she could make out Adam asleep at her side. She took a moment to study his beautiful body, her gaze roving from his handsome face to his big chest on down to his abs. When she reached his cock, her eyes widened. *Damn, how the hell is it still so big soft?*

She turned away from her lover's perfection and slid to the end of the bed. A moan rose to her lips at the soreness between her legs and the ache in her back. She squinted at the far wall, expecting to see cracked plaster, but there was none. In fact, no one had come to complain about the noise they made, so she guessed the next room lay empty. Thank goodness for small favors.

Uttering tiny yelps, she made it to her feet and took a tentative step. The nightstand took most of her weight while she sucked in a breath. She worked her way to the wall and used it to inch along. Thank goodness the bathroom was situated on her side of the bed. She didn't think she could make it from Adams's side.

At last, she stepped onto the cool surface of the bathroom floor and then decided to run a bath rather than take her normal shower. The hot water went a long way toward easing the sore muscles, and she soaked until all the warmth faded. Tempted to run another bath, she resisted and brushed her teeth, washed her face with the morning cream she liked, and then brushed her hair. The tangled heap seemed a bit worse for wear after last night's sexfest, but she could stand to wait until she returned home to have a stylist get it back to its usual luster. For now, she drew it into a ponytail and snapped a band into place. When all morning rituals were completed, she walked into the bedroom, plotting how she'd find clothes before Adam had the chance to see her naked. Her girly parts needed recovery time, and another session with him would kill her.

The bed lay empty.

Sakura blinked. Her eyes must be deceiving her. She scanned the room and checked for the clothes Adam had left in tatters on the floor. He had never left after they had sex. Always, they enjoyed breakfast together and spent most of their days in each other's company for work and for pleasure. Adam leaving before she came out of the bathroom made her feel cheap and used, and she didn't appreciate it. Never mind the hurt his actions evoked. She suppressed those and vowed to let him know what she thought of his treatment when she saw him next.

She walked to the table to look for her phone and remembered Adam had swiped everything to the floor. She found her phone under a chair and looked at the time. One thirty in the afternoon. Next, she checked the messages. No calls or texts from him, but Roger had phoned twice and left a text asking her to call him. She pressed her lips together and blinked to clear her vision. After the emotions died down, she called Roger.

"Sakura," he blurted as if he'd been sitting by the phone. She smiled. Well, that went a little way to soothing her pride.

"Hey, Roger. Sorry I missed your call."

"You were busy, I guess." He paused as if she'd fill him in on her activities. She said nothing. He cleared his throat. "Um, I wanted to see if you'd have lunch with me. I have to apologize for last night."

"What happened wasn't your fault, Roger. If anyone deserves an apology, it's you. How is your nose? Did the doctor say it was broken?"

"I'm fine. It wasn't as bad as it looked."

"Don't try to act all macho. I've seen tons of broken noses in my line of work. Adam wasn't himself last night. He hurt you, and I'm so sorry. If you talk to my dad, I know he'll pay all your medical expenses, and if he doesn't, let me know."

"All I need from you, beautiful lady, is a lunch date. How about it?"

She rolled her eyes. "We can do lunch. How about half hour? Meet me in the lobby?"

"Sure. See you there."

She dressed, thinking about Roger and Adam. By the

time she was ready to go downstairs, she'd made up her mind. There was no future in a sexual relationship with Roger, and she would tell him so. She never kept men hanging around, wondering—well, unless the job required it. As far as Adam, she needed to drop him. Things had gone too far, and since he wanted to marry her, it was unfair to lead him on. The problem was it hurt to let him go. Then again, maybe his leaving her room without saying anything meant he now felt the same. Last night could have been his good-bye. A lump rose in her throat at the thought, but she swallowed it and pulled her attention to the coming meeting with Roger. One man at a time. *For now.*

Sakura left her room and headed to the elevator. When she reached the ground floor, she found Roger leaning against the reservations desk chatting up the attendant. The Latino woman blushed prettily at whatever he said to her, and Sakura raised an eyebrow as she approached. Amusement transformed to shock when Roger turned toward her. There wasn't even a bruise on his face let alone a broken nose. He produced a toothy grin, waved good-bye to the attendant, and led Sakura out of the hotel. On the pavement outside, she paused rather than get into his car.

"What's the deal with you, Roger?" she demanded. "I expected a broken nose."

"You wanted me to still be hurt?" he asked, his innocent gaze annoying.

"Of course not. You know what I meant. Don't play games." She put her hands on her hips and leaned in close to him, examining his face. She froze, her mouth falling open. "Oh crap. Do you have makeup on?"

He spun away and opened the car door. "You make a habit of chopping off a man's balls, Sakura?"

She stuttered over an apology and then chuckled as they got into his car. "Yeah, I guess I do. Really, I'm sorry. I practically yelled it for the whole world to hear, huh?"

He kept his gaze locked on the street ahead of them, but she knew from the stiff set of his shoulders and the tightness in his jaw she had embarrassed him.

"For what it's worth, it looks good," she offered, but knew the words sounded lame.

"I got the swelling to go down with ice, but I was still bruised. I went to a drug store asked the lady there what I could use to cover it. She suggested something called concealer and gave me the one for my coloring. It worked."

Sakura grinned. "Looks hot. No wonder the font desk clerk blushed all over herself."

He glared at her, and she laughed again. "I really am sorry."

"Don't!" He groaned. "Listen, if you want to make it up to me, you and I can pick up where we left off last night."

"Sleep with you to make up for my ex punching you? Um, no. My body's worth a lot more, pal."

"Your ex?" He eyed her and signaled to make a right turn. "He didn't act like an ex. Then again, maybe he did. Some people don't accept when it's over. Come to think of it, you called him Adam. Is that Adam Martinez, your protector?"

She stiffened. "Yes, so?"

He pulled to a red light and stopped the car. "Adam Michael Martinez, born in Puerto Rico, raised here in

Miami. Half Puerto Rican, half Cuban. Adopted by an aunt who was investigated many times for neglect, but nothing came of it."

"Stop," Sakura spat. "I know you looked into all of our backgrounds, but I don't want you reporting on Adam's life as if he's just another name in your database. Yes, he had a difficult upbringing. I already know that. He practically raised himself, and when he was old enough to go looking for his mother, she said she didn't want him. You can't imagine that kind of rejection. For that matter, neither can I, so I'd appreciate it if you kept your mouth shut about Adam."

He blinked at her outburst and then turned back to the road. "I didn't mean to offend you. I apologize."

Sakura could kick herself for her words. Adam didn't hide his background. He didn't care who knew of his struggles. He had risen above them, but for her to defend him in the way she had, as if she would take Roger's head off for even mentioning it, gave away too much. There must be no doubt in the man's mind she had unresolved feelings for Adam. On top of that, she realized she had been insensitive asking him to come to Miami with her. The city must have bad memories for him, and he had already told her he didn't come home often. When she spoke to him again, she would make it right, and then talk to her father about reassigning her someone else as protector.

After an awkward period, she and Roger chatted again. They ate lunch together, Sakura enjoying his company without any motives. To do so with a man felt pretty good, and she smiled at him without reservation.

She flirted, and half way through their meal, she sighed because the man seemed to hang on her every breath. Without meaning to, she'd used the wiles she had honed over the years to trap many shifters. Roger being a regular man was no match, and she considered how she would extricate herself from his expectations without hurting his feelings. After all, she had been harsher than she intended earlier.

"Sakura," he said, toying with his glass of wine.

She tensed, hoping another invitation to bed wouldn't follow. "What's up?"

"I have some information I'm not sure about. I wouldn't bother sharing it until I did some more digging, but since we're here…"

She frowned. "Come out with it, Roger. What do you mean?"

"A possible shifter sighting."

"Give me the details. I'll go check it out."

He hesitated and then looked into her eyes. "It's a woman, a very beautiful woman."

"Oh."

"Usually the men handle the women, don't they?"

She nodded. Why was he still being so damn cryptic?

"I know for a fact she flew in late last night. I know where she's staying, but I didn't go by there. The hotel. She's under an assumed name, I'm guessing because I couldn't find out any details on her other than the flight she came in on originated in Texas. No trails beyond that."

"So what makes you think she's a shifter?"

"A tip."

"What kind of tip? From who?"

He sighed. "I can't give up every single source."

"And why not?"

"I haven't confirmed everything. Remember, I'm building the database. When it's done, I'll add everyone to it—everyone who *wants* to be added. Some like their anonymity."

Sakura rolled her eyes. "Whatever. But I understand you want to be sure. How about I go feel her out a little? Like you said, we're here, and if there is a female shifter, I want to get my family involved so they can send someone to deal with her. Of course, if I determine she is and I have the opportunity, I'll take her out. Period."

Roger flinched. Again, she was reminded the man didn't belong in the field. He could never handle her as a lover. Sometimes she came home wanting to vent, to unleash some of the stress, and Adam had listened to every detail of what she'd done, even though he'd been there with her. He understood her ritual kept her sane. Roger would never be able to deal with the violence of her job, even hearing it second hand.

"I'll go with you," he said, surprising her.

"No, you won't."

"Sakura, you don't have a protector."

"Adam is in Miami."

"Where is he now?" he insisted.

She clamped her teeth together. Despite everything, Roger had sensed her confusion over Adam. He might even realize she wasn't ready to talk to Adam, let alone take him on a job. She kept assuring herself she'd call and get things straight, but a part of her wanted to put that talk off. *Besides, I saw him just this morning. I'm not procrastinating.*

"Fine. You can go, but you'll stay in the car. No arguments. Got it?"

He nodded.

"Let's go now. No time like the present."

After he settled the bill, they left the restaurant, and Roger handed her a slip of paper with the name of the hotel where the woman stayed. "The Acqualina?"

Roger led her to the car and held the door for her. "Yeah, she's got an oceanfront suite there. Only two thousand dollars a night."

Sakura shrugged, and he blinked at her. She chewed her thumbnail thinking. "What's she doing here? Meeting someone? Damn, I messed up. I usually handle this better. I killed that guy without knowing if he had family or friends like him. She might have had a connection with him, or there may be others."

"Maybe," Roger said. "It's still worth it to go check her out though."

"Of course. I want to have something concrete to tell Dad."

The moment they stepped into the Acqualina, Sakura regretted her more modest but still posh hotel choice. Across the lobby at the check-in desk, a guest had just turned from handling business when a waitress appeared seemingly from nowhere with a tray of drinks. She murmured a few words to the guest, and the guest nodded and took what looked like a cool tropical beverage. She sipped it, smiled in relief, and the waitress disappeared. A bellman whisked the woman's luggage toward a bank of elevators while the woman followed at a leisurely pace.

"Stay here. I'm going to work my charm," Roger told her.

"Boy, please, everyone is not going to fall for that smile of yours."

He winked and strode away. The next thing she knew he returned, and she smirked at him. "No go?"

"She's not in her room at the moment but at the spa. This way." He gestured, and Sakura resisted popping him in the back of the head for the self-satisfied air he wore. They headed down a corridor and made a few turns until they reached a small room decorated in rich hazel and cream. Soft leather couches and white candles burned on the tables giving the atmosphere a relaxing feel, and the attendant behind the counter spoke in soothing tones. This time, while Roger engaged her in conversation, Sakura pretended to examine the bath oils on sale. When the woman turned her head, Sakura slipped beyond the counter toward the back. She was met with a row of closed doors and frowned. Short of opening each door to check out who lurked beyond, she considered her next move. Voices around the corner reached her, coming closer, so she pressed her ear to one of the doors, and hearing nothing, ducked inside. The room lay empty except for a bed, a counter with various bottles lining it, and stacks of towels on a shelf. A set of buttons on the wall controlled lighting and music, she deduced by the labeling. Another door at the opposite end of the room caught her attention, and she went to investigate. So far, the decision to come wasn't working out. Her mind wasn't in the game. Under normal circumstances, all arrangements would have been made. She would have only to arrive as a guest and soon hobnob with her prey, no need to sneak around at all.

The door turned out to be locked, so she returned to the one she used to come in. A listen at the panels produced no sounds in the hall, so she took a chance and opened the door. One after the other, she listened to each door, not knowing what to expect or what she would hear. When she neared the end of the hall, she started coming to the conclusion that she'd just tell her dad about this woman and go back to her own investigation. Then the deep timbre of a familiar voice stopped her dead in her tracks.

"Aw, don't be that way, suga'. I know you were with *her* last night," said a woman with a saccharin-y sweet voice and a strong Southern drawl. "It's my turn now."

"*Maldita sea*, Laila! We're not having sex here," Adam said.

Chapter Six

Sakura froze. She stared at the door as if she could see through it and then backed away. All the while, she felt her mouth hanging open, but she was at a loss to how to close it or get a grip on herself. Pain tightened the muscles in her chest, and betrayal echoed across her skull. *Stupid, stupid, stupid,* she chided herself in silence. She had no right whatsoever to feel the way she did, and yet tears flooded her eyes and fell down her cheeks. She was blind to where she walked, but she spun around and charged forward anyway. She had told Adam in the beginning they would never be exclusive. He accepted that, but the moment she fell for him—and damn everything she *had* fallen for him, *hard*—she dumped all other men. Sure, she kept up the pretense that any day she might pick up a new man, but the truth was, she couldn't. Her heart no longer belonged to her. Accepting the fact had been near impossible, so she had turned down his proposals one after another. He had every right to be with whomever he chose. The problem was, up until today, Adam had chosen only to be with her.

She scrubbed her face just before entering the spa's lobby area.

"Ma'am, you're not supposed to be back there," the attendant scolded. Sakura ignored her.

"Sakura, what's wrong?" Roger asked. She ignored him, too.

She kept walking, past the two people staring at her, out into the hall, to the hotel's lobby, and out the front door. Roger caught up with her and grabbed her arm. He turned her to face him, and as many times as she blinked, she couldn't bring his visage into focus.

"What happened back there?" he asked.

"Nothing," she muttered and pulled from his grasp. "I'm... I need some alone time. I'll get back to my hotel by myself. Talk to you later."

"I don't feel comfortable letting you go off like this."

"That's not your choice, is it?"

He flinched at the vehemence in her tone, but she didn't have the ability to be nice. If she stood there with him much longer, she'd either attack him or throw up on him. Neither appealed, so she ran away. Never in her thirty-three years that she could remember had Sakura Keith ever run away from anything or anyone.

She kept moving, until she left the driveway and reached Collins Avenue, then turned left. Leaving the luxury hotel, Adam, and Roger behind her, she half walked, half jogged. After a while, her throat burned, a stitch lit up her side, and her feet hurt. She slowed her pace but didn't stop. After a stop at Walgreen's on Collins and One Seventy Fourth Street for a bottle of water, she set out again. The busy traffic started to get to her, so she cut through a path alongside some condominiums to the beach. There she slipped out of her shoes and squished her toes into the sand. Near the water's edge, the sand was cool, and she shut her eyes.

"Hey, beautiful, want some company?"

Sakura opened her eyes to meet the hungry gaze of an over-tanned man in swimming trunks and nothing else. The way he stood made it obvious he sucked in a slight paunch. She gave him a pointed glare. A slow blush crept up from his chest to his face, and he turned away. She thought she heard him let go of his breath. She found an available umbrella with a lounge chair beneath it and curled up on it. Eventually, the sun slid below the horizon.

Sakura leaned back in the chair and tucked an arm behind her head. A shadow moved in her peripheral vision, but she paid it no mind. Not far away, parties swung into high gear as if people used the night as an excuse to act like they had no sense. Music echoed across the water, along with shouts of laughter and cheers. Soon the shadows lengthened, and she let the swish of the waves coupled with the merrymakers soothe the raw pain.

"Found you," someone whispered out of the gathering darkness.

She leaned up and scanned left and right. No one lurked nearby, but then something zipped from behind, and a hand covered her mouth. She tried biting down, but the man knotted his hand in her hair and jerked her head back. She rammed an elbow backward but impacted with air. Using her weight against him by rolling to the side didn't produce the results she had expected. He stayed with her. When she hit the sand on hands and knees, he flipped around to lie atop her, crushing her into the soft earth. *Bad move, Sakura. You're in real trouble.*

"Do you know what I'm going to do?" he asked, his tone too low to recognize. A tongue along the side of her throat followed the words, and she gagged. He chuckled at her response. "Not that. You have a dirty mind."

She mumbled "fuck you" against his palm but doubted he understood it. Scouring her mind for some way of getting free or at least calling someone's attention to her plight, she waited for his next move. What he did next took away her ability to think let alone fight. His teeth sank into her skin, deep, sharp, and very painfully. A cry wrenched from her throat. Although she and her family had speculated, none of them could have imagined what it felt like be changed and to endure the pain spreading fast throughout her body, and ensuring she would never be the same again.

Sakura woke on the beach with the sun shining down on her. She lay beside the lounge chair, now turned on its side. A woman stumbled along, holding shoes in her hand, makeup smeared, hair a mess. She met Sakura's confused gaze and offered a small smile.

"Better get moving before they catch you," the woman slurred.

Sakura tensed, and fear made her heart pound, but then she realized the woman probably referred to the authorities. She guessed everyone assumed she slept off a strong hangover rather than being the victim of an attack. Remembering her ordeal, she reached a hand to her neck and found—nothing. On her top, the only evidence of the night's events was a small stain of red. Her skin remained unbroken. Could she have imagined it? Maybe being upset with Adam had thrown her so much she started hallucinating.

"Can I go now, lady?"

She jumped and looked to her right. A young man, early twenties at least, stretched out beside her. Sakura took in his scruffy clothes, his scraggly facial hair, and crinkled her nose at his obvious body odor. The man looked pointedly down, and she followed his gaze to find her fingers curled around his arm in a grip so tight bruises under it were obvious.

"Wha…" She gasped. "You attacked me!"

"No, I swear, I didn't." He tugged at his arm, but she held on. Fear widened his eyes. "Please, it hurts."

She looked between them and spotted her purse. She realized her wallet hung half way out of it, and she guessed what happened. This man had tried to rob her while she was unconscious, and then what? She licked dry lips.

"What happened?" she said in a hoarse whisper.

"I um…" He rubbed the back of his neck, sitting up. "I tried to see if you were okay and you grabbed me. I tried all night to get away, but you held on. I've never met a woman so strong. I thought you were going to crush my bones."

"And you didn't yell for help?"

He flushed.

Sakura opened her fingers slowly, and as soon as she did, the man scrambled to his feet, fell in the sand, and rose again. He ran full tilt down the beach and disappeared along one of the paths around the side of a hotel. Left alone, Sakura gathered her purse and frowned at all the sand inside. She searched her wallet and found all money and cards present. The blinking light on her cell phone caught her attention, and she checked the messages. Several calls, voicemails, and texts from Adam. None from Roger. Without listening to or reading any, she tucked the phone in her purse and stood to look for her shoes.

The journey to her hotel blurred in her mind, especially with thoughts out of control of what happened to her—what was still happening, from the burning in her arms and legs to the churning in her stomach. Her tongue felt too big and her teeth sharper, but when she reached up to investigate with her fingers, everything seemed normal.

"I'm imagining it all."

Thoughts of the way she'd held that man for hours came to mind. No amount of training would give her that level of strength. A new idea presented itself while she used her key card to enter the suite. Perhaps she had been poisoned as she thought, and it wasn't a shifter turning her. She smiled with the hope that this was true, but paused just a few feet into the room. A deep breath burned her lungs, and her purse slid from her fingers. Her legs gave, and she dropped to one knee. Scanning every surface, she judged whether anything had been moved and decided nothing had been. Unfortunately, this didn't change the certainty that Roger had been in her room. His scent filled her nostrils, and she moaned in anguish. Roger's natural aroma was wholly male and pleasant, but it was hardly strong. He didn't wear overpowering cologne, so why the hell could she smell him?

She found the strength to stand and strode deeper into the room. A square of the hotel's notepaper lay on the end of her bed. A smiley face had been drawn in the middle. Atop it was a scribbled message. *"Call me. R."*

He could have dialed her cell or texted her. He had the number. The sneaky devil had decided to worm his way into her private space instead. Why? Pissed, she crumpled the sheet and tossed it into the garbage, then returned to her purse to grab her cell. With fingers poised over the keys, she froze as realization of the truth came flooding through.

Roger came to the room to show her he could, to remind her of his scent, and to nail a particular fact home. He was a shifter, and whatever kind he was, now, so was she!

Chapter Seven

Adam frowned at his phone. No calls. No texts. He toyed with the idea of phoning Sakura again but changed his mind. If she'd wanted to talk to him, she would have returned his call. He knew she was pissed. After all, he'd left the room without even waiting for her to get out of the bathroom, but he couldn't explain how he had no choice in the matter. The night before last, he'd been close to crossing the line. Desire like he had never known drove him to take Sakura's body and use it for his own pleasure. He had never treated her that way and never wanted to again. Yet, even now thinking about her, he'd give his left nut to have her writhing beneath him.

Maldita sea, calm down, Adam.

Arms roved around his waist, and large breasts flattened against his back. He stiffened, clenching his jaw. "How did you find me, Laila?" he demanded.

She chuckled, and he extricated himself from her hold then stepped back. She tapped her nose. "This is very good."

He glared. *"Qué demonios estás hablando?"*

She squealed like a schoolgirl. "Oh, I love when you speak Spanish, and your accent gets me wet. What did you just say?"

He drew away when she tried to latch onto him again. Not that Laila Stark wasn't beautiful. She was. Long tresses of silky black hair flowed around slender shoulders. Wide, green eyes gave an air of innocence that he'd learned right away was deceiving. One might assume her to be in her early thirties, but she bragged to him the first day when he met her that she passed forty-five six months back. Confidence oozed from every pore, but what annoyed him more than anything was the Southern belle wanted him in her bed, and she never stopped trying to seduce him.

"It means what are you talking about," he supplied with long-sufferance in his tone, hoping she would get the message.

"Oh, well it sounded sexier. Never mind that. When are you going to stop playing hard to get, Adam? The two of us could have a lot of fun between the sheets. Us bears have some hot blood running through our veins. We can hardly stand a day going by without getting our needs met, if you know what I mean."

He frowned. "I'm sure you can have any man you want."

"Yes, I can." Her words were pointed as she stared at him, meaning, he assumed, it was a matter of time before he gave in to her. He admitted what she'd said to him was true. His sexual desire bordered on obsession. A beating of his cock in the shower that morning had done nothing to ease the ache.

"I want one thing from you," he said.

Her expression turned sultry, and long false lashes lowered. "You can have it, baby. Any time you're ready."

She came at him, but he grabbed her shoulders, squeezing too hard. She winced, and he let up with an apology. "I feel like I'm out of control. Like just now, I hurt you, and this burning desire all the time. I can't think straight. Not to mention how I feel like my head will explode if I get a whiff of perfume."

Laila laughed. "It will even out after a while. Most of it, anyway. The sex drive will be manageable but still pretty high. That doesn't matter. All you need is another shifter to handle you."

"I don't need to be 'handled'. Thanks."

A hip jutted out with a hand above it. Her dress seemed to grow shorter, showing off long, shapely legs. "Then handle me."

Adam sighed. "I already have someone."

"We can share, or better yet, a threesome."

His eyes hurt he widened them so much. Allow anyone else to touch Sakura, even a woman? *Not happening!*

His distaste must have reflected on his face, because she laughed again. "Well, are you going to turn her? You know it only takes a bite or a good scratch. Every shifter doesn't have the ability to make new ones, but we do."

"Not unless she wants it," he said, thinking about Sakura. Would she even accept him as he was now? He had been desperate, determined to show her strength she could not deny, but now with emotions raging out of control, and the way he had made love to her the other night, he'd be lucky if she didn't drive a knife into his heart.

"I want to meet with the woman. Maybe I can answer any questions she might have."

Suspicion rose in Adam at her words. He didn't trust Laila not to hurt Sakura, and if she realized who Sakura was, there might be more trouble. The only reason his maker accepted him in the first place was because of Birk, and he had been surprised the man hadn't told Laila about Adam's associations with the Keith family.

"You're not meeting her," he said.

Laila bristled. "You don't trust me."

"Why should I?"

She gathered her purse and headed for the door of his hotel room. "You know where I'm staying. Call me."

"What about these..." He hesitated, embarrassed. "Urges."

Her hot gaze flitted over his body, lingering at his crotch. "The only urge I'm interested in helping you to explore is the sexual one. The rest you can figure out. Just don't kill a human and get caught."

The door slammed behind her.

He blew out a breath of relief that she'd gone and picked up his phone to call Sakura. He'd done so automatically despite his earlier decision to wait until she contacted him. After checking the time, he decided enough was enough. They needed to talk, if only for him to apologize for treating her the way he had. If she didn't want to listen, too bad. He'd make her hear him out. Thinking that way brought him up short, and he searched his intent. Sure, anger surged within him, but unlike the warning Laila gave about killing, he felt no push from the beast within to do harm to Sakura. If anything, the creature chomped at the bit to get near her again, to smell her, to touch her body.

"*Maldita sea*, Adam, cool it!" He spent a few moments rolling his head around on his neck, breathing deep, and thinking calming thoughts. When calm reigned—or the best it could get—he set out to Sakura's hotel. A short time later, he stepped into the lobby of the hotel where she stayed and could swear he smelled her. The distinct scent teased his nostrils and yet, it seemed different. Maybe it was his imagination. He shook the doubt away, headed up the elevator to her room, and knocked on the door. He waited. No answer. He dialed her number, and no ring sounded from recesses beyond the door. Frustration drove him to find someone to let him in, and he located a bellman. After he stepped over the threshold into Sakura's room, he wondered if it was the aggression of the beast or the large tip he'd given the man that gained him entry. Either way, he decided to hurry in case the man contacted the authorities.

Sakura's room lay in perfect order, her bed made. He checked the bathroom and found no wet towels. Either the maid had been in or Sakura hadn't returned to her room. He thought of the little jerkoff he'd found coming onto her and ground his teeth. A deep breath through his nostrils brought in several different scents. He had no idea how he knew and could distinguish between them. He dismissed the ones he identified as food and focused on Sakura's and one other. The man whose nose he had tried to shove into the back of his head had been here.

Sharp pain brought his hand up to his mouth, and he realized in his anger his teeth had sharpened and cut his tongue. Blood stained his palm. *Calm, calm, calm,* he chanted in silence. He'd changed once after Laila bit him, and it had been the most violent feeling he had ever experienced. He had no wish to repeat it in the middle of a hotel room.

Why wasn't Sakura here? She was not an early riser unless work demanded it. Why wouldn't she answer his calls either? Even angry, she was more likely to cuss him out rather than avoid him. This wasn't like her. Had she run into trouble investigating her mother's death? Worry niggled in his gut, and he balled his hands into fists. Once again, the bear raised its head by changing his fingernails into sharp, dark claws. He uncurled his fingers slowly, watching as the claws pulled out of his flesh. More blood. Pressing a wad of toilet paper against the wounds, he considered his next move. Perhaps he could use Laila's technique. Had she really smelled him all the way from Texas? He chided himself for his naivety. More likely she had connections that allowed access to local flight lists. The Keiths had a few of those as well, so it wouldn't surprise him if a shifter found a way.

He removed the toilet paper to find his skin healed, if stained with blood. After a quick wash and dry, he turned back toward the room and froze. The unmistakable scent of the man who wanted Sakura had grown much stronger, distinct enough he had no doubt the dude lurked outside Sakura's room. A moment later, Roger walked through the door and stopped cold at sight of Adam in the bathroom entryway.

"Where is she?" Adam growled, aware his voice had gone deeper and more threatening.

Roger eyed him, his gaze assessing. "Why would I know?"

Adam wasn't aware he had moved until he had Roger by the collar and slammed him against the wall. Plaster cracked, and the smaller man coughed, the air having forcefully left his lungs, but he made no move to counter Adam's attack. Flaring his nostrils in sharp dislike brought one fact home to Adam. Roger's face carried no blemishes, not even a bruise.

"Your nose," Adam said, confused.

"Yeah, funny about that," Roger said, a tight smile on his face. "Uh, mind letting me down?" He wiggled his feet, and Adam glanced down to find he'd raised the man more than a foot off the floor with one hand. His own strength startled him, and he let Roger fall to the floor. Roger sprang to his feet and put space between them.

Adam turned, facing him, ready for attack. He studied Roger from head to toe. "You're not human!"

"Just figuring that out?"

Adam started for him, but Roger raised his hands in surrender.

"Whoa, guy, I don't want to fight you. We both know who would win. I promise. Sakura is not with me."

"Your word means nothing."

"I realize that," Roger said. He edged toward the door as if Adam didn't see him. "How about this, then? You're Adam Martinez, right? Sakura's protector? You work for the Keiths. I wonder what Sakura and her family will think to learn you're no longer human."

The words were scarcely delivered before Roger disappeared. Adam could have sworn he would be able to catch the man before he got out the door, which was why he made no move. The sneaky fuck was fast and much swifter than Adam would have believed. He wondered just what type of animal Roger was. Adam believed he knew the scent of a bear, any type of bear was yet to be seen, but he had no clue of Roger's beast identity without prior knowledge.

He didn't worry about Roger telling the Keiths about his change. The family meant little to him. Only Sakura, and maybe her sisters. If she didn't reject him, it might be possible for them to reconcile, but that matter was for later. Right now he needed to locate Sakura to be sure she was safe. He considered asking Laila about how to track her but decided against it. Instinct seemed to say he could find Sakura no matter where she was on the planet. What he didn't know was whether it had to do with how much he loved her or something different, something to do with the bear. Either way, he intended to find her soon.

Chapter Eight

Adam sat in the rental car watching the building where he had tracked Sakura. Her scent led beyond the gates, but he had hesitated to pursue her inside because of the armed guard. The sign on the building referred to this being a textile company, so why such high security? He didn't buy it, and he didn't like it that whoever ran this place had the woman he loved in there with him. All Adam waited for was night to fall, and then he would enter—guard or no guard. They would not know what hit them.

A text buzzed on his phone. He dug it from his pocket and read the display.

"Please, answer the phone, Mr. Martinez, for Sakura's sake." The bottom fell out of his world. Seconds later, the phone rang, and of course, he answered.

"You have three seconds to explain yourself before I find you and I kill you," he said.

Sputtering on the other end of the line was quickly covered with a cough. Then the man spoke. His nasally pitch grated on Adam's already thin nerves. "Please, calm down, Mr. Martinez. I assure you we will not harm Ms. Keith. We only want what's best for our own kind."

Adam assumed the man meant shifters. He might be one of them now, but he felt no allegiance, certainly not when they had Sakura. "Where. Is. She?"

"She's safe. I notice you're parked outside our facility. If you will come up to the guard and give your name, he'll let you through. That's better than storming in in your shifted form, right? Potentially drawing the authorities?"

While Adam didn't care if the police knew about these people, he didn't want them knowing about him. He'd likely be hauled into some lab and experimented on, and that would mean he couldn't protect Sakura. For now, he would play along.

"Who am I speaking with?" he demanded.

"Deveron Montgomery." The line went dead.

He turned over the car engine and drove up to the guard's box. After he'd given his name, the guard raised the barrier and waved him through. Adam gripped the steering wheel until the leather squeaked, but he kept his gaze swinging side to side, looking for a trap. No one appeared until he had parked outside the main entrance. When he walked up to the door, a man unlocked the door. Adam stepped through and almost choked on the stench of fear. He pierced the man with a narrowed gaze.

"T-this way." The man gestured toward the end of a long, dark hallway. Apparently, everyone had gone home for the day. Maybe all the humans, he surmised, because he scented quite a few shifters like his escort. While they walked, Adam allowed one side of his mouth to quirk upward. The guy refused to walk directly in front of him but chose rather the left side with way more space between them than necessary. He probably thought Adam would attack. Good, let him think that. He welcomed the fear and intimidation he produced in hopes it would get him answers. If the peaceful approach didn't work, he would give in to the beast. The question was, would he come back from it without Laila's help?

They turned a couple corners and then came upon a large conference room. Several men sat around the table, all watching with intensity as he passed the floor-to-ceiling glass until he reached the doorway. His escort darted into the room and almost ran to the opposite side of the table. Adam stopped to take them in. Every one of the twelve men present were the same animal, even as they appeared to be of various ethnic backgrounds. More than half were white men. Adam rolled his shoulders and fixed a steady gaze on each individual. He let the contained aggression that simmered on the surface come through loud and clear. To his surprise, most were not afraid, but they were cautious.

"Please, Mr. Martinez," a man with a familiar voice said, and Adam realized he was the ringleader from the phone call. "Have a seat here. Can I get you refreshments, some coffee maybe?"

"This isn't a social call. I'm here for Sakura. Why can't I smell her anymore? What did you do?" He advanced on the man, and the people nearest took a step back.

"She's not at this site," the man said. "Like I said, we're not going to hurt her. Mr. Martinez, please, if you take a seat, we can get down to business."

Adam ground his teeth. "Stop with the damn Mr. Martinez. *Me llamo* Adam."

"*Lo siento,*" came the response, and Adam blinked.

"I deal with many of your people in business, so I'm fluent in your language. If it makes you feel more comfortable, we can converse in your native tongue."

"Forget it," he snapped and decided to take a seat. He was outnumbered, and while he knew he could do major damage before anyone took him down, it wouldn't necessarily help him find Sakura.

The scent hit his nostrils before the platter plunked down in front of him. Adam squinted at the pastries. He was not too fond of sweets, but enjoyed a hearty meal. To keep his body strong and trim, he worked out, and he sparred with Sakura. The time he had bested her in her house and made love to her afterward seemed years ago.

"Please help yourself," Deveron said.

Adam didn't understand it, but he found himself tempted beyond reason. He scanned the men's faces, wondering if they'd poisoned the pastries, but Deveron smiled and took one. He bit into it and soon downed the sweet. Another man poured coffee for everyone. Before Adam could say a word, he heaped a mound of sugar in Adam's cup.

The scent too much to resist, Adam selected a dessert and took a tentative bite. No odd taste or reaction came over him—unless one counted the feeling of being in heaven. Pastry after pastry disappeared into his mouth, and he didn't stop until he reached for another and found the platter empty. Sharp embarrassment made him scoop up the coffee and drain the cup. He cursed, glaring at Deveron.

Deveron laughed. "I put nothing in it. We're not in the habit of harming our own."

"I'm not like you," Adam growled.

"Not exactly, no. But you *are* a shifter. A bear, right?"

Adam hated that they had the advantage. "And what are you?"

Another man spoke up. "Maybe we should keep that to ourselves, Deveron."

"No, no. We want Mr...I mean... We want Adam to trust us, so it's important to be transparent. We're foxes."

Adam blinked, disbelieving.

"Show him." Deveron nodded to the man who'd insisted they keep their secret, and the man frowned. He obeyed though, walking around the table and into the open space to Deveron's right. Adam stared wide-eyed as the man's suit fell to a pile on the floor. Beneath it a small lump wiggled, and soon the small head of a red fox appeared.

"Estas brutal!" Adam shook his head.

The tiny furry animal disappeared beneath the pile again, and soon a very naked man stood in its place. Adam turned away and heard the rustle of the man dressing.

"Also," Deveron said, "for your information, the reason you enjoyed the pastries so much is because one of the main ingredients is honey. Bears enjoy eating young bees, and because of it, develop a taste for honey. It's not some made up trait from a children's story."

His calm explanation did not make Adam feel any better. To think he would eat anything as disgusting as a bee was preposterous, but he had proven the theory of bears enjoying honey. He shoved the plate away. "I don't care about honey or what you think you know about me. What I want to know is what you think you'll do with Sakura."

"Nothing."

"Explain!"

Deveron steepled his hands together, elbows on the table. "It's very simple, Adam. Sakura Keith, the oldest daughter of the well-known Keith Hunters, is now one of us. And if my sources are correct—and they are—she was the last of the darlings. Shae Keith is a wolf shifter, and her sister Shiya is in a mated relationship with two bear shifters. The Keiths are essentially no more. We shifters are now at the top of the food chain."

Adam stood slowly from his chair, his gaze lowered to the table to hide the violence bubbling into overload. He leaned forward and grabbed Deveron's shirtfront and dragged the man halfway onto the table. Cries of alarm rose throughout the room. Adam bared teeth he knew were razor sharp, and when he spoke he didn't recognize his own voice. "Did you bite her?"

"N-n-no, of course not. I would never," Deveron stammered. He was no small man. In fact, Adam would put him at similar weight and height to himself, yet Adam held the man without effort. Deveron swallowed, his Adam's apple bobbing up and down. Deveron named a man Adam didn't know.

"He acted on your authority though, right?"

Deveron paled. He seemed to search for soothing words, and then his expression cleared. Two heavy hands slammed down on Adam's shoulders and drove him into his seat. Against his will, he had to let go of Deveron, and the man stood and straightened his jacket. A pleasant grin creased is face.

"Thank you, Savino," Deveron said.

Adam strained to see behind him and caught sight of a burly man at least six and a half feet tall, shoulders that must fill a doorway, and a scarred face. The blemish ran from mid left cheek up over his eye and disappeared into his hairline. From the staring quality of that eye, Adam guessed Savino saw nothing through it.

"I'm sorry I was a little late, sir," Savino said with a lilt to his voice. Adam guessed him to be of Italian descent, and from his very nonhuman scent that he too was a shifter, but definitely *not* a fox.

"Look, Adam," Deveron said, "we wish you no harm. All we want is to take back control from the Keiths, to ensure none of our people are hunted down and slaughtered ever again. The stronger shifters did nothing but hide. We, the foxes, considered weaker, came up with a plan."

"What kind of plan?"

He shrugged. "To take down all the Keith women for one, and that's pretty much been done. It's obvious you can't return to the family, but understand if you even try, we'll be sure to expose you for what you are."

Adam sneered. He fidgeted beneath Savino's hold but realized if he wanted to get away, he'd need a full on fight with the big man. "You instill such a feeling of trust with that threat."

"I'm sorry, but it's necessary. Now that you understand

our position, you may leave anytime you wish. Savino, let him go." The pressure disappeared from Adam's shoulders, and he flexed. When he stood up, so did every other man in the room. Savino watched him as if poised for attack should Adam threaten Deveron again. "You will see Sakura very soon. The fact is there is an adjustment period for her to gain control of her emotions. We want her to be in a safe and comfortable environment while she learns."

Adam thought of his feral sex drive. "If anyone touches her—"

"No, she's your mate. We recognize that."

Mate. Adam swallowed his questions and nodded. After a few more comments from Deveron and one or two of the others, Savino showed him the exit. Adam walked back to his car, anger pulsing through his system. He felt no satisfaction at how he behaved back there, nor had he any guarantee the foxes would release Sakura when she was ready. He hated being away from her, but instinct said if he couldn't trust Deveron, he at least knew the foxes meant her no harm. They considered her one of them, a fox. He slid behind the wheel of his vehicle and shoved hands through his hair. Two different species of shifter? He had been worried about whether she would allow him to turn her, but this. With no idea what lay in store for his relationship with Sakura, he started the car and drove back to his hotel. They had better not keep him waiting long.

Chapter Nine

Sakura hated them all, every last one of those damn foxes. The cliché was that foxes were sneaky, and Deveron Montgomery was as sly as the animal any day of the week. He smiled at her, pretending to be agreeable, but all the while, but he was self-serving. They wanted to use her, keep her with them, but even if she were no longer human, she'd be damned if she helped the animals come against her family. With her constant threats to kill anyone who stood in her way, Deveron had at last given the order to let her go. Some weird giant of a man drove her back to her hotel, and all she thought about on the way was finding Roger to kick his ass and finding Adam to demand an explanation.

"Thanks for the ride," she muttered to the scarred man whose name she had dismissed as fast as whomever had mentioned it to her. He nodded a thick head, pale eyes solemn, and drove away. Sakura walked into her hotel. She hadn't been there for a few days, but she wasn't worried because she had paid up through the end of the month.

Deveron had told her before she left he would be in touch. He had given her his cell number, but the man could hold his breath for her call. In the elevator headed up to her room, she began to pace. The shaft stopped on a random floor, and a man stepped in with her. Sakura spared him a glance. The higher the car rose, the more she fidgeted, and she didn't know why. A longing ache came over her, and she found herself close to a whine. Frowning, she did a mental walkthrough of her state of being. The woman she had stayed with while held by the shifters had taught Sakura to shift completely into a fox. Her assurance had been that doing so would relieve Sakura of a lot of the pent-up energy, which seemed to come with her new makeup. She'd informed the foxes she had no wish to embrace this—*beast*—but found they were right. The full change helped, and she had regained a bit of sanity. Now she wondered if she needed to do it again and that was why she was almost out of her head in this elevator.

"Are you okay, miss?" the other passenger asked.

To Sakura's—and the man's—surprise, she snarled at him. He jumped back, flattening himself against the elevator wall. She spun away, embarrassed and cursed whichever of those cowards had bitten her. Deveron had refused to tell her which one, probably knowing she intended to relieve him of his life.

The moment the doors opened, she dove out of the elevator and then became crystal clear why she'd lost control. Adam's scent assaulted her nose in a powerful wave. Aching, desperate need tore through her system. Rational thought disappeared. All she knew was an undeniable drive to climb into his arms and demand satisfaction.

Her hands shook as she shoved the key card into the slot. She knew he stood just beyond the door. His scent overwhelmed her senses, and when she banged the door against the wall, having used too much strength, she leaned out to grab it but missed. Instead, she tumbled into his embrace as if he'd been waiting for her. Adam snatched her purse from her hands and threw it on the floor. He gathered her off her feet in a bear hug that threatened to crack a rib. When her feet left the floor, she let her shoes fall off and wrapped her legs around his waist. His mouth descended on hers, and she parted her lips to receive his tongue.

A moan escaped them both at the same time, and the hungry, greedy kisses filled the room. Adam's hands slid over her ass, and the material of her dress seemed to disintegrate beneath his touch. Material ripped, panties shredded. He was inside her before she knew what happened, pumping deep and hard while they stood by the entrance. Sakura banged a hand on the wall to support herself. Adam gripped her hips, squeezing into her flesh with strong fingers, and drove his massive cock deeper. She cried out his name against his lips. Then a memory hit her. Drunken from his loving, she shoved at his chest and climbed down from his hold.

"Wait, wait."

"Sakura," he groaned, and the sound contained agony, but he let her go.

She took a step back, panting, struggling not to mount him again. "You were…" She drew in a deep breath. Her hand rested in the center of his chest, and she took in the sight of him, all solid muscle and perfection with an aroma of raw male sexuality that made her head spin. She licked her lips, staring at him through a slitted gaze and tried to recall what she intended to say.

"…with another woman."

"Never!"

His sharp denial was followed by his big body pressing her into the wall, a knee between her thighs she found hard not to hump. He thumbed her chin up and crushed her lips in a hungry kiss. When he raised his head, his eyes were darker, much darker than they had ever been. A niggling of something passed over her consciousness, but she couldn't pin it down.

"You are the only woman I want." He brushed her hair away from her forehead with a rough hand and kissed her again. When he let her breathe this time, he traced the curve of her jaw, down to her throat, and he let his teeth graze her neck. She stiffened, having no idea if he broke the skin if it would make him like her. She needed to tell him the truth about what she was, but seeing rejection in his eyes was worse than death.

When did he become so important to me?

"Adam."

His muffled voice vibrated against her neck, and the warm breath tickled. "Let me in, Sakura."

She spread her legs, and he dipped his knees. His cock slid home inside her pussy as if it belonged there.

This time around, her body accepted him, stretched to take every delicious inch, and while it ached a little, she felt sure she could take him all night and be no worse off in the morning.

Sakura fell silent, and Adam drew back. She almost protested, but he did so only to stare at her bare breasts, cupping them with a feverish light in his gaze.

"You ruined my clothes. I'll have nothing to wear."

"Fine by me. I love you naked."

She glared at him, but Adam missed it because his attention lay on her breasts, swollen and pushing against his palm. She thought she heard him chuff, but desire must be making her hear things. Adam dropped to his knees and pressed his face to her belly. He stuck his tongue out to taste her flesh, and she moaned. When she looked again, he had slipped lower, his mouth poised before her wet pussy.

"What are you doing, Adam?"

"Smelling you."

The ragged words made her think he spoke Spanish at first. He buried his face in her trimmed muff and breathed deep.

"I'm the only one that touches you, Sakura." He leaned back and tapped above her mound. "If I smell another man here, there will be trouble."

Her eyes widened, and then she put a hand on her hip. "Excuse me? Is that a threat? Because I think you forgot who you're talking to."

He slid his hands up from her calves to the outside of her thighs to her hips. A lave at her clit sent a shiver coursing through her body and heated her blood at the same time. Adam's belligerence hadn't lessened when he met her gaze again. Her anger did not faze him. "My threat isn't for you, Sakura."

She got it then. He would hurt any man who dared touch her, but what was it he'd said? If he even smelled a man on her? "Adam what did you mean—"

He covered her pussy with his mouth and began to eat, laving and sucking until her knees buckled. She whimpered, the words slipping away from her lips. She wanted to grasp his head and drive him harder against her throbbing clit, but the strength to do so ebbed. Her arms hung limp at her sides while he ravaged her pussy. He moaned, sending vibrations to her core. He stuck his tongue inside, scooped the dripping come, and wiggled the tiny muscle around. She called out his name and arched into him, riding his mouth until an orgasm roared through her core. Adam didn't rise from his spot on the floor until he'd licked up every drop of her cream.

"Turn around," he commanded, "and catch the wall."

She did as he said but looked over her shoulder to watch as he removed the rest of his clothing. Her mouth watered at the glimpse of smooth, taut skin, rich with a natural tan but a bit darker after spending such a short time beneath the Florida sun. He moved close to her, staring down at her ass as she poked it out toward him. His cock strained to reach, and the thick head just touched her cheek. Adam guided it along her rear and dipped his knees. One hand on the wall, the other holding his cock, he arched, and his shaft parted her folds to glide deep into her channel. She rolled up to her toes and curved her back to take all of his offering.

"You need to understand something, Sakura," he whispered, and his lips caressed her shoulder. "This is mine. *Mine.* I will no longer share you. Ever. *Entiendes*?"

She said nothing, but concentrated on the feel of him inside her.

"Sakura," he ground out. "Do you understand?"

"You act like I have no choice." She moaned at the pleasure he gave her. Already another orgasm built.

"Do you think you do?" His hand came around her waist to flatten on her belly. He drove in, pulled out, and then ground in hard and fast. She shook from head to toe, the sensations so strong she let them resonate all over her body. The sounds they both made, the feel of him, his scent, took her desires to heights she could not deny. So when he asked her if she thought she had a choice, she knew the answer without a doubt.

"No. I don't."

His hand slid down over her navel, and he parted his fingers around his cock, feeling it slide between them and into her. The pressure from the heel of his hand on her clit felt too good. She came, but she wasn't sure when it started and if it would ever end. Adam made a sound in his throat, but with her eyes closed and confusion reigning, she wasn't sure if he crowed with triumph. Not until his hot seed spilled inside and seeped down around his shaft to coat her upper thighs. Adam held her in a bear hug, and she nuzzled his neck, loving him more than she loved anyone, and she knew in that instant she could no longer turn him down if he asked her to marry him.

After a few moments catching their breath, Adam pulled out and raised her in his arms. She laughed. "You are always carrying me to bed."

"That's bad how?"

She stuck her tongue out at him, and he set her down. Before he had a chance to join her, the truth of what she realized earlier hit her between the eyes. Panic, confusion, relief, and myriad other emotions juggled across her consciousness.

"Adam," she murmured, and he froze, a knee on the bed.

"You're not..." She licked her lips. "You're not human anymore."

Worry creased his brow, and he sat down, abandoning what she knew was his intention of lying beside her. She felt the loss as a punch to her stomach.

"No, baby, I'm not." He pushed fingers through his short-cropped hair, messing it up worse than it already was. He still looked insanely hot. "I'm something else. Different from you."

"Different from—" She gasped. "You aren't surprised I'm not either."

He frowned. "Deveron Montgomery informed me."

"Deveron? That bastard. I should have dealt with him when I had the chance."

Adam chuckled.

"This is not a laughing matter."

He stroked her cheek but dropped his hand to his side when she stiffened. "I admit I've had slightly longer to get used to the idea, and I know this is a huge loss for you with your family, but it's not all bad, and it doesn't have to change our relationship. In fact, you saw just now. You can take me better than you did the first time."

She blinked. "You were already a shifter the last time we had sex? That's why your dick was so huge."

The bum had the nerve to look pleased with himself. Sakura stared him down, and he shrugged then stood up. He walked into the bathroom, but she followed him. He wasn't getting away. While he stood in front of the mirror wetting a washcloth, she took in his form. The scar on his lower belly was still there, puckered and darker than the rest of his skin. She remembered him telling her when he was seventeen another boy mistook him for someone else, a target he had to take out as initiation into a gang. Adam had fought for his life but still ended up hurt. While he recovered in the hospital, his aunt hadn't come to see him once. She'd been too busy with her own life. Adam had vowed then to get out of Miami, and he had worked several jobs to do so. He visited infrequently.

Sakura moved next to him and smoothed fingertips over the roughened skin. "Becoming a shifter doesn't fix this."

His amused gaze met hers in the mirror. "You have a problem with how my body looks, *mami*?"

"Yeah, right."

His muscles were harder, firmer. For that matter, so were hers. Not like a man's, of course, but she did have greater strength, and it blew her mind. There was also the fear of what the future would hold cut off from her family and disgust that something not human crawled around inside her.

"Adam, what are you?" she asked. He didn't answer right away.

"Tell me what you think of yourself."

Her eyebrows rose. "What do you mean?"

"Sakura, you don't like depending on anyone, but there was always the security of your family behind you. When they learn what you are, all that will change."

"It doesn't have to. They can't smell shifters, you know."

"So you'll go on killing your own kind?"

"They're not my kind!"

He said nothing, and she sighed. His arms came around her, and he guided her back to the bedroom. They lay in the bed together, Sakura snuggled to his side. She breathed in his scent. Definitely wild, not a fox, and if she had to guess not a small animal either. Adam would die before he let someone turn him in something like a rabbit. At the thought she almost laughed, but a lump rose in her throat.

"I don't know what I think or feel. I'm a little..." The word *scared* stuck and refused to leave her mouth. "I'll handle it."

Adam's lips quirked. "Don't be scared. Even if they reject you or try to hunt you when they find out, you know I'll be there to fight for you."

"You'll always be my protector, huh?"

"It's not a job for me."

"About that 'no man can touch you' stuff. It sounded kind of dangerous."

He raised his hands and tucked them behind his head. Sakura stared at him. She didn't want to miss anything he might be hiding, because it was for sure Adam hadn't told her everything yet. He stalled about admitting the type of animal he shifted into, and that worried her.

"I'll put it simply for you," he said, looking up at the ceiling, but she caught the dangerous glint in his gaze. "I will rip off the head of any man who touches you, whether you let him or not."

"That's violent even for you."

"It's not me."

She sat up and wrinkled her nose at him. "What's that mean?"

"Did you notice a certain trait to the people who had you?"

"Oh, you mean like sly, sneaky, cunning." She rolled her eyes. "I can go on."

He nodded. "*Si*, like that."

"So the beast in you is a killer?"

"Never!" He sat forward and drew her into his arms to stroke her back. Sakura submitted to a few kisses but then pulled away. She wanted nothing to interfere with his confession. Adam let her go with reluctance. "We were taught the shifters have mates, another person who is meant for them, who are sealed to them, in a sense, for life."

"Yeah, I never got that. I thought it was all BS."

"What do you think now?"

She decided not to pretend. "We're mated, and nothing can stop or break it. I feel like we're a part of each other."

"I'm glad you admit it."

She punched him in the chest, and he pretended it hurt.

"Sakura, my beast is the kind that would hunt the earth looking for his mate and find her. Period. He will kill without remorse to keep her safe. Nobody had to tell me that. I know it. The emotions from that desire are, I guess you can say…intense. I haven't controlled them all the way yet, so I'm asking you. I'm *begging* you, let me be enough."

"You already are, and you've been for a long time, even before we changed." She turned away, but he drew her around again, capturing her attention.

"Sakura."

"Yeah?"

"I'm a bear."

She opened her mouth to make a quip but snapped her teeth together a second later. A bear shifter, like Shiya's lovers? Had they done this to him? She frowned, thinking she should have gone to Juneau to kill them long before now. "You're telling me you are a polar bear shape-shifter, and right now if I asked you to, you could change into this massive beast with white fur all over your body?"

He blinked at her, and then his expression cleared. "I'm not a polar bear. Let me explain from the beginning."

He told her every detail of his trip to Alaska, his conversation with a man named Birk, and his flight to Texas. Sakura had a problem when the story turned to Laila, and she told him so. "She wants you. I heard her propositioning you in that spa at the Acqualina."

"You were there?"

"You didn't smell me?" She smirked.

Guilt reflected in his expression, and Sakura was ready to go find Laila. "She kept pushing. I was dealing with a lot. Remember I told you about the emotions? They were out of control. Trust me, I smelled you everywhere, so if I picked up your scent at that hotel, I thought it was a figment of my imagination."

"Well, just like you, Adam, I don't want her touching you. I'll make it clear you're mine real quick."

"She's a bear, Sakura. I don't want you provoking her."

"And what? I can't take her because I'm a lowly fox?"

"I didn't say that."

"You didn't have to."

He drew her onto his lap, straddling his hips. Since they were both still naked, her pussy pulsed being inches from his cock, and she dared not look down because something told her he'd gone hard.

"I know you can give her a run for her money, and she would come out of a fight with you wounded or dead. I've seen you in action, remember? But we haven't come across a lot of large animals, and every time we did, I was there. You have to admit, they're harder to take down. Laila is—*we* are—grizzlies."

"A—A grizzly." Her mouth fell open. She thought of the predatory animal that even the smallest ones at three hundred pounds could run off a twelve hundred pound polar bear. Birk hadn't turned him.

A storm of emotions swirled through Sakura's head, not to mention the probabilities and possibilities of being mated or married—or whatever one wanted to call it—to a grizzly bear. In nature, she would be his lunch.

"Not to mention kids," she murmured, tugging at her hair.

"What?" Adam caught her hands and brought them down to her sides. His gaze left her face and traveled to her belly as if he imagined it swollen with his child.

"Don't even," she grumbled. "We're too different."

"That was your excuse before we became shifters."

"No, it was that I saw you as the newbie I helped train. Now you're—"

"Too far above you?"

She rolled her eyes at him, and he laughed.

"You're loving this, Adam, but I'm serious. We can't risk having weird mutant children who are half bear, half fox. That's creepy and gross."

He seemed disappointed. "We'll work through everything. There's time. Meanwhile, how is your investigation going?"

"It's not. I've learned nothing. No, that's not true. I learned where my mother was killed, but that's all. Everything went to hell fast, and I haven't had the chance to find out more."

"Well, you've got me now. We can figure it out together. *Esta bien?*"

She nodded. *"Bien."*

Chapter Ten

Adam stood behind Sakura's chair as she shot off an email to her dad. He frowned. "Are you sure about this?"

Sakura paused in typing, her lips moving as she reread the wording she'd chosen. "We already figured out Roger's left Miami. I don't know if he's headed back to San Diego or what. Either way, he's not what the family thought he was. They should be warned. I'm not going to say he's a shifter—although I can't explain why—but I'm telling Dad not to trust him. He'll believe me and be more cautious when dealing with Roger. You better believe though when I catch up to him, his ass is mine."

"All right, it's your call. We have more than enough to deal with here. The hunters can handle themselves. I got us an appointment with the medical examiner's office at three."

"Mm, you're so resourceful."

He shrugged. "I charm when necessary and threaten when it doesn't work."

Sakura peered at him over shoulder. "Which was it this time?"

"I'm not telling you."

She laughed, and he was glad for her good mood over the last couple of days. While they had planned to get moving on the investigation, they had hardly stirred from bed. When they had, they had discovered Roger fled Miami. Adam noticed a couple fox shifters watching them when they did venture out, but Sakura made no indication she knew, and he had no reason to tell her. As long as Deveron and his men kept out of his way and stayed away from Sakura, he didn't care what else they did.

That afternoon, Adam took Northwest Fourteenth Street, which sat off Twelfth Avenue and continued to Northwest Tenth Avenue, also called Bob Hope Road. Once he'd turned onto that street, he passed the Miami Transplant Institute and kept driving until he reached the building that housed the Medical Examiner Department, Records Bureau. After slipping into a parking spot, he stepped out of the car and jogged around to hold the door for Sakura. She quirked an eyebrow at him, but offered a slight smile. If he didn't know any better he would think his mate was happier and freer than she had ever been. Was it the fox that did it or his change? Either way, he figured she would not admit the truth should he broach the subject, so he kept his observations to himself. For the moment, he decided to enjoy this new Sakura and help her solve the mystery around her mom. When it was over, well, he had some plans formulating in his mind, which he believed would work out great for the two of them.

They walked into the building and located Transcriptions, the secretary of which scheduled appointments for the medical examiners. The unit also produced reports for autopsy protocols, neuropathology, and microscopic exams. During his conversation with the secretary, she had shared that the building housed two research rooms should any research be needed. His mind had produced all kinds of scenarios for what one could study within these walls, and most of them made him cringe in disgust. What he never wanted to see now that he was one of them, was studies done on a shifter. Then again, this probably wasn't the facility for it. A shifter might be sent off to some secret lab in DC.

Adam touched Sakura's arm to signal her he would do the talking this time around. He expected annoyance, but she acquiesced and stepped aside. The pretty blonde smiled at him, and he returned it with caution, sensing rather than seeing Sakura stiffen. "Hello, I'm Adam Martinez. I believe we spoke on the phone. I have an appointment with Jon Stine."

"Of course, Mr. Martinez, I remember you." The chirpy voice had dropped low and sultry. Adam caught Sakura's forefinger just before she raised it to point at the woman. He kept her tight to his side, and she frowned at him, but he kept his gaze on the blonde.

"Yes, before we see him, I wanted to ask you about any records you might have on file for Yvonne Keith."

The woman swiveled to her computer. "If the incident

happened after nineteen ninety, then we have the records here. If it's between nineteen fifty-six and nineteen eighty-nine, then they're off-site, and I need a few days to get access to them. Plus, I'll need you to put the request in writing."

Adam waited with limited patience while she ran through procedures he had already familiarized himself with. He found it comical she called the murder an "incident" and rushed to inform her the death had occurred well after nineteen ninety. Soon they were handed a bunch of papers, and Adam sat down with Sakura to peruse then. Right away, he saw there was missing data and glanced at Sakura.

"There's nothing about the bear attack," he whispered, careful not to allow the human to hear. He frowned. When had he begun thinking of himself as anything but human, separating himself and Sakura from the secretary? Was it part of a self-awareness that developed the more time passed?

"It doesn't have anything in here about the stab wounds," Sakura commented. "There are whole chunks missing. All of this is useless!"

Adam stood and approached the secretary. "There's missing paperwork here, and there's not one picture included. Do you have anything else on file?"

The blonde shook her head, curls bouncing. "I'm sorry. That's it. I don't know where the rest could be. We keep meticulous records. We have to because often they're depended on for depositions in court. I shouldn't admit it, but I checked the computer, and there's even less there. It's weird."

"Thanks." Adam turned away. No, it wasn't weird. Hiding shifter existence was the name of the game with both the Keiths and shifters themselves. The original report from Kasen Keith, Sr., Sakura's dad, was that he'd found Sakura's mother dead, the apparent victim of a bear shifter attack. Had the shifter been there at the time, and did Kasen Keith kill him?

A short while later, the medical examiner entered, and Adam stood to shake his hand. Jon Stine seemed like a reasonable man with nothing to hide, yet it could be an act. Adam and Sakura walked with him to his office and sat down.

"Can I get either of you some coffee?" Stine asked.

"No, thank you," Adam said. He got straight to the point. "What can you tell me about the...uh..." He glanced at Sakura. "Body of Yvonne Keith? Anything unusual?"

Stine appeared to check his notes. Adam had informed him of whom they were coming to discuss and gave a plausible cover story that Stine seemed to accept. As a part of his previous work with the Keith family, Adam kept false credentials in support of Sakura in case he had to get into places that were off limits.

"When you called, I checked the database and the physical records, and I found a lot of information missing. I don't understand it," Stine said, and Adam's hope faded. Stine continued. "However, I like to keep my own personal notes to add my thoughts. The file on my computer is missing, but I have a paper backup. I'm old school." He winked, and Adam sat forward, interested.

"So you do have information?" Adam prompted.

Stine opened a desk drawer and pulled out a file folder. He opened it, and Adam saw that several photocopies of pictures lay stacked inside. He handed a few to Adam and some to Sakura. Then he held up another to show them. "If you see here, here, and here." He pointed with his little finger to several spots along the wounds. Adam checked on Sakura and found her lips tight. She appeared paler than usual.

"Okay?" he whispered. She nodded. Adam didn't think she was, but he knew she would never admit it. He longed to take her into his arms or at least to hold her hand, but neither of them wanted Stine or his people to know her true identity. If she were simply a colleague of his as he had indicated, there was no reason she should have an emotional response to the pictures.

"Go on, Dr. Stine," Sakura encouraged.

"The wounds are consistent with a sharp object, probably a knife or a sword."

"A—A knife?" Sakura choked. "But I was led to believe they were caused by a..." She coughed. "An animal."

The man frowned. "No, I'm sure of this. Besides, how would an animal that could do this much damage get into a motel room, unless someone put it in there?" He stroked his jaw. "I suppose that *could* happen. I've seen stranger situations in my line of work. Desperate people perform desperate acts to cover their tracks."

"Is there anything else you can share, sir?" Adam asked.

"The wounds are precise, too ordered, as if they were made cover something."

116

Adam thought about it. Someone could have made the knife wounds to cover a shifter attack. That wasn't unheard of, but why take away all evidence as if it had never occurred? Why provide a cover for a shifter kill then throw in more suspicion by making that evidence disappear? Unless by looking into the murder, Sakura had stirred a sleeping enemy who wanted to hide his involvement. While she had arrived under a false identity, at least one set of shifters knew who she was, and they had made use of their knowledge by making her one of them. On top of that, Roger with a foot in each world—both in the Keiths' employment and a shifter himself—could have informed any number of others of her presence in Miami. Then he disappeared before Adam could question him. *Or wring his neck.*

Adam stood. "Thank you for your help, Dr. Stine. I greatly appreciate it."

"Of course." Dr. Stine stood as well. "I'm thinking it might be a good idea to reopen the case."

Adam stiffened. That had not been their intention.

"Unfortunately, I don't have the resources or the time. The most I can do is pass on my suspicions to the lieutenant who headed up the initial investigation and let him make the call. Trust me when I tell you there are more cases like this one than I care to admit. Well, I wish you luck in your search for answers."

Stine shook Adam's hand again, and after Sakura expressed her own gratitude, Adam escorted her to the exit. Neither of them spoke a word until they were in the car. Sakura was the first to speak. "Do you think they did it to hide that they were responsible?"

He knew she meant shifters. She hadn't accepted what she was just yet. "It's possible, but whoever did this had to know your family would call them on it. Did your dad ever say who specifically did this?"

"No, I don't think he ever had a name. He and the men with him just hunted the guy and killed him. End of story. The beast's background didn't matter to any of us. My dad made sure we all realized how dangerous shifters are. Believe me, as hard as it was to look at a picture of my mom, it did fuel my hatred to kill every last one of those fuckers I came across."

He tightened his grip on the steering wheel. "Do you still feel that way?"

"Don't ask me that, Adam."

"Okay, how about we visit the motel you found?"

She looked at him. He still didn't like her coloring and the obvious strain in her beautiful sienna gaze. "Why would we go there? I told you the room has been cleaned out, probably reused."

"It might be pointless," he agreed. "But you were human the last time you visited, and so was your dad."

Sakura gasped. "You're right." Then she frowned. "But it's been five years. Would there be anything left?"

"Can't hurt to see."

"Okay, let's go."

They arrived at the motel not much later, and Adam frowned in doubt. At his side, Sakura chuckled.

"Told you it wasn't much."

"I agree." He slipped his hand in hers and gave her a gentle tug when she started in the direction of the office. "Let's handle this ourselves."

They headed up, and Sakura kept a lookout while he jimmied the lock. He had the door open in minutes and stepped inside. Myriad scents assaulted his nose, included among them some kind of cleaning agent. Adam frowned and shoved a fist against his nostrils. Sakura stepped in behind him and looked at him.

"You okay?"

"This doesn't bother you?" he said, voice muffled.

"It stings a little. I think they cleaned it recently, like in the last day or two." She turned to press close to him and raised her chin. He found his attention arrested by the sight of her soft lips, and she tossed him a saucy look as if she knew the reaction to his libido. "I guess that means your bear outdoes my fox."

"My bear will *do* your fox any day," he quipped.

"Ew, you're gross."

He chuckled and moved out of her hold in case he gave in to sudden urges, and tossed her on the narrow bed. After circling the small room a couple times, mentally preparing himself, he lowered his hand. The cleaner still burned, but he endured it to try to pick out anything else. "Humans," he murmured, "a cat, maybe two."

"Shifters?" Sakura said, surprise in her tone.

"No, housecats. Probably. Weird I never thought I could pick one out, but these scents are stronger. There are others that seem thinner, barely there."

"Older," she supplied. "I think maybe new ones overpower them or they fade with time. I can't believe you're picking them out like this. I can smell it, but I just don't know what I'm picking up. You're pretty impressive, bear."

Adam strode past her on his third circle of the room and smacked her ass. She let out a yelp that made his bear raise its head. For an instant, his vision changed, and all he saw was Sakura in his sights. Although he blinked, it was as if the bear didn't care about anything else except claiming her. Her scent and hers alone filled his nostrils, tantalized him, driving him to follow when she zipped away nearer to the bed. Adam put his hands out about to push her down on the soft surface and lay atop her.

"I just want to know what really happened to my mother and put this behind me for good." Her words, filled with hurt she worked to hide, stopped him cold.

"We'll find out. I promise."

She moved away, and he breathed a sigh of relief. His head began to clear, and he saw the room again. This time, a subtle scent tickled his nose, and he crouched by the bed, going still so he could concentrate. "Deveron," he growled, and Sakura gasped behind him. He dipped his head and shut his eyes, allowing himself to breathe a bit deeper, ignoring the cleanser. "That big guy. I've forgotten his name."

"Savino? What do you know? I do remember."

He turned to look at Sakura. "You've met him?"

She nodded. "He brought me back to the hotel after they let me go. I don't know what he is, but he's not a fox."

"Neither is he a bear." He turned back toward the bed and shut his eyes again. "I smell one, maybe two, of Deveron's men, plus the leader himself and Savino. They've all been here. What I don't smell is a bear, but

I'm not entirely sure I'd recognize all species of bear. Laila told me there's a similarity in all same species, such as any type of bear, and I have no reason to doubt her."

"Of course not."

Adam pressed his lips together, amused. His sweetheart was jealous. She had no reason to be. "So it looks like Deveron's people wanted to give the impression your mom was killed by a bear. They knew the Keiths would never be fooled this wasn't a shifter attack. Now all we have to do is crack a few heads to find out which one of them did it."

He stood and faced Sakura. She'd removed the knife she carried in a holster on her thigh. "Crack heads? Please, I'm going to gut a fucker and ask questions afterward."

Chapter Eleven

Sakura had lectured herself the whole time they sat with the medical examiner. She teased Adam while they were at the motel, taunting him, knowing it would drive him nuts and make him want to go back to her hotel room and get a little afternoon fun in. None of it made any difference to her state of mind—worse, the emotion caused a lump, which felt like the size of a baseball in her throat. From the moment she saw the pictures, all the memories and the hurt, the confusion, and anger came flooding back. Sure, she let the anger drive her to do her job, but getting lost in the maelstrom that they were could drain a person faster than anything. Exercise, medication, and just self-talk helped her through it all five years ago, and now here she was, about to meet with the man who might have been the cause of her mother's death.

Her stomach stirred, and when Adam suggested they stop for lunch, she had turned him down. She'd seen the way he looked at her, suspicion in his eyes, but she had forced a smile and said something joking. He had offered a courteous chuckle, but she knew she wasn't fooling anybody. In the way her lover held the steering wheel and the tension around his sexy mouth, she figured he understood how close she was to falling apart.

"Think he'll see us?" she asked, as a way to distract herself from her thoughts.

"He'll see us."

She touched Adam's arm and sensed everything he felt. Not that she could smell it or read his mind. She just knew. The two of them felt connected on a level she never even heard of, let alone experienced, and something told her Adam knew everything she felt, too. She drew her hand away as if he'd burned her and turned her head to look out the window. Familiar street signs met her gaze along with landmarks that said they neared the building Deveron brought her to that first morning after she woke as a shifter. Savino had knocked on her door, and when she answered, he explained his mission. Sakura had known this giant of a man was not human, and while she guessed he could crack a man's jaw with one hand, she somehow sensed he wasn't there to hurt her. Wanting to get answers and find out the name of the bastard that turned her, she'd gone with him. Who knew the change would almost break her mind and exhaust her body before she gained a semblance of control. In the end, Deveron had told her he'd sent the man who attacked her away, probably to keep her from killing him. With that experience, she wondered if he would cooperate now. Why would he?

"Adam, pull over!" She slapped a hand over her mouth and shut her eyes. Her head spun, and she swallowed convulsively. Adam slowed, and she shouted, "Pull the hell over, please!"

He almost climbed the curb, but Sakura didn't care. She had the door flung open in a heartbeat, and her feet pounded on the asphalt.

"Sakura, stop," Adam called, but she kept running.

She knew she looked a sight, hair flying all over her head, face tight with emotions threatening to erupt at any moment, huffing it like a serial killer were on her tail. Blood pumped in her ears, so she couldn't hear if Adam gained on her until he shouted something in Spanish. The next instant he grabbed her arm and slung her around to face him. She didn't think the man knew his own strength so when she yelped, he eased his hold. Sakura fought him, trying to push him away.

"I can't. I just can't do this again, Adam. I can't!" Her voice rose, and she felt tears but refused to let them fall. Her chest heaved, throat burned. "You don't understand. I've lost them *all*. Every last one of my family. They're gone, and I can't get them back!"

"Sakura, look at me." He cupped her face between two large hands and forced her to meet his gaze. "I'm going to take care of it. You hear me? I'm going to take care of it."

She tried pulling out of his hold but failed. "I don't need you to fix it for me, Adam. I keep telling you that."

He sighed, and she saw frustration in the set to his mouth. "Then we will both do it. You're going to get your family back."

"That's impossible."

"You *will*."

She said nothing.

"Now, we're going to go back to the hotel for a few hours."

"What?" She wrenched away and glared at him. "I'm fine. We can go see Deveron."

"We're going to the hotel."

"I said—"

"Sakura! You're too upset. You were taught just like I was about going into a job cool-headed so you don't make stupid mistakes. Tell me I'm wrong." When she didn't answer, he turned her back toward the car, and Sakura walked woodenly at his side, staring straight ahead, feeling lost and confused. Adam tucked her into the passenger side of the car and shut the door, then sprinted around to his side. When they arrived at the hotel, she made no move to get out but waited for him. He tossed the keys to a valet and curled her into his side as he guided her up to her room.

Sakura stood in continued silence while Adam stripped her down to panties and bra and tucked her into the bed. She followed his movements with her eyes as he shed his clothing and slid in the opposite side of the bed. The mattress dipped under his weight, causing Sakura to roll toward him. He opened his arms, and she landed against his chest. Burying her face at the base of his neck, she pulled in several deep breaths. A tremor rocked her body, and she balled her fingers into fists, fighting it, hating weakness, but feeling like at that moment her emotions buffeted her about with no regard to her mental stability. The pathetic truth was she'd kept her family at a distance. So how could it devastate her now? Why break down at this point after she had a couple days to realize the full impact of her changed life?

The pictures. She had seen the picture Kasen, her older brother, carried with him everywhere he went as a reminder of the violence of shifters, but seeing the others at the medical examiner's office, the various angles, close-ups, and then having to pretend it didn't matter. That got to her, and she had done what she had kind of been doing for the last five years—run.

"I'm sorry," she mumbled into Adam's warm skin. She thought his body temperature might be hotter than before his transformation. "I didn't mean to lose it back there."

Adam stroked her hair. "You're human. It happens."

"No, I'm not."

"You know what I mean."

She rolled over, and he drew her against him, circling an arm about her middle. She covered his hand on her belly, and felt almost as if he fed her with his energy and strength. "Adam, this scares me. I think about knowing the whole truth, and then I think about not knowing. A part of me wants to go find a country far from the United States and stay there."

"Then I'm torn between following you and making you stay to face this."

"I've been selfish."

He touched her chin, and she twisted around a little to look into his curious gaze.

"Since you got here, it's been all about me. Do you want me to go with you to visit your aunt?"

He frowned. "No."

"Adam, she's family."

"You're my family, and when this *lío* is over—this mess—we'll have more family again. I have no doubts about that."

She studied his face, wondering if he meant kids because she intended to let him know they weren't having any. No way. She used protection, and it was her choice whether she came off it.

Adam appeared amused.

"What?"

He shook his head. "*Nada.* I can just see inside your head."

"Whatever."

"Feeling calmer?"

She gave herself a mental check and nodded. He took her hand and tucked it beneath the sheets, laying it on the front of his boxers. Sakura wasn't surprised to find him hard as a rock. She'd seen the glances cut to her breasts. They swelled above her bra because of lying down, and it turned him on.

"A quickie?" he suggested.

She gave him a squeeze and then rubbed his cock's length through the thin material. Adam moaned, and his eyes closed. Thick, dark lashes rested on his cheeks, and she lamented seeing them on a sweet baby that looked just like him.

Get that thought out of your head, Sakura. Ain't happening.

Adam took her touch as encouragement, and she moaned when he stuck two fingers into the crotch of her panties and ran them along her slit. He breathed deep.

"Smell that?"

She did, her own musk, moisture gathering in anticipation of his entry. Adam pushed the sheets back and leaned up on an elbow. He liked to look at her naked and had insisted on leaving the lights on from day one. She had never minded because she worked hard to keep her figure. Sakura spread her legs for him, and he explored farther inside her panties, the curve of his hand rising and lowering along her snatch.

"Mm, you smell good enough to eat." He dipped a finger between her folds, and it sank into her heat. She moaned, lifting her hips off the bed. "Like that?" he teased.

"Yes, your knuckles..."

"Are they hurting you?"

"No." Her voice came out breathy. Adam's knuckles bumped her clit, and it felt like her undoing. She couldn't claim his sex drive was too high. She wanted this as badly as he did. Her pussy throbbed for him to mount her, fill her, and pound out orgasms until she couldn't take it anymore.

Adam pushed his fingers deep, withdrew, and then glided in again. He wiggled the digits around, and then took the experience up a notch when he used his other hand to tug back her bra and capture her nipple between his lips. Sakura trembled, moaning and pleading for more.

He looked up at her while tantalizing the stiff peak and pleasuring her pussy with his hand. Sakura bit down on her jaw, and a tightening began in the center of her belly. More come slicked along his fingers, and Adam looked, an eyebrow raised, and clicked his tongue.

"So wet for me, *mami*. Do you want me to make you come like this, or do you want my cock inside you?" He didn't give her the chance to answer but sped up the assault on her throbbing kitty. She squirmed and moaned, one minute grabbing her knees to open up to him more, the next squeezing his hand between her thighs. She humped his digits and held his wrist. The pleasure skyrocketed, and every time he sank into her moist depths, she thought she would lose it. Her core muscles contracted, released, and then coiled again. She arched and grabbed her panty line to be sure it didn't get in the way of her pleasure.

"I can't take it," she shouted. "I've got to come."

"Do it, baby," he murmured. He closed his lips around her nipple and sucked hard. Her world flew apart, and she screamed loud and long. Adam made a sound, and the next thing she knew he stood in the corner far away from her, half turned, his eyes wide. He ran hands through his hair, and when he brought them down, Sakura gaped. She licked her lips.

Adam's skin rippled, and she thought the color fluctuated. Clawed fingers rested on the wall, and she heard the paper covering tear as he tried to close his hand. His mouth open, he shut his eyes and dipped his head.

"Adam?"

He pointed at her but didn't look her way. When he spoke, the gruff quality to his voice surprised her, even as she expected it. "Stay there."

She moved to her knees and climbed off the bed. "Adam, calm down. You can't change in here."

"Don't, Sakura. I don't want to hurt you."

"Do you feel like you will?"

He didn't answer, but she wasn't letting him torture himself. She took a tentative step toward him, and a growl erupted in his throat. She paused, waiting, and then moved again. Adam's gaze swept her from head to toe. The obvious need radiated off of him. Somehow this time around he had gotten too excited watching her rather than satisfying his own lust. They were both so new at this with no direction from anyone else. Mistakes were bound to happen, but if she knew anything she knew Adam loved her, and he would never hurt her, even in his bear form.

Still moving with caution, she crossed the room to stand in front of him, her arms at her sides so as not to startle him. His breath came in heavy pants, and now that she stood closer, she made out the beginning changes. The bear looked out from dark brown eyes, and she could have sworn they were just a little closer together than usual. Fine, almost black hair smattered across his chest, which hadn't been there before.

Adam opened his mouth to tell her to move back, and she spotted the overlong, sharp canines. Fascination made her reach up to touch, and Adam stopped her, the long claws circling her wrist.

"Sakura." Her name on his tongue held a tormented quality, and she leaned into him, resting a hand on his chest. He groaned, and his cock twitched between them. She pressed closer, and he released her wrist to grasp her at the hips. Slowly, the signs of the change receded, but when he still would have pushed her back, Sakura dragged his boxers lower to free his erection. Before he could stop her, she dropped to her knees and took his length in her mouth. Salty precome coated her tongue, and she sucked him deep and then let his cock slide out. She licked the underside and circled the head with the tip of her tongue. A shudder passed over Adam. He laid a hand on her shoulder, but she refused to be put off. She held his cock at the base and looked up at him.

"You're my mate, aren't you?"

He swore.

"I'm going to make you come, Adam. It's what you need, and no other woman can satisfy you like I can." She grinned at him. "Remember that."

"I can't control…" He bit off his words when she put him into her mouth again. She took him deep, feeling the head touch the back of her throat. Pressing down with the roof of her mouth, she sucked hard. Adam chanted, "Fuck, fuck, fuck! Yes, Sakura!"

She palmed his ball sac and massaged them, careful to be gentle. Knowing he liked it, she let the juicy sounds of her devouring him mix with hungry moans. Adam sagged against the wall, and she followed, not letting him go. For long moments, she worked his pole, loving him, pleasuring him, and when he stiffened, and the breath hissed between his clenched teeth, she knew he was ready to blow. Seconds later, hot come filled her mouth, and she met his feverish gaze as she drank it down.

Sakura leaned away and swiped the back of her hand across her mouth. She stood. "There. Better?"

She turned away, but Adam's arm snaked out, and he

hauled her backward to his chest. He bent his knees, lining hard thighs with the backs of hers. A hip pivot brought his shaft up between her legs and into her pussy. He gave a mighty thrust, and her nether lips stretched around his thick girth. She'd just gotten him off, but he was still this hard?

Her head fell back onto his shoulder, and her eyelids fluttered closed without conscious thought. "Adam, *mm*."

He thrust hard and fast, controlled as he trapped her in a steel embrace. Her feet left the floor, and she marveled at his strength, holding her while he pounded his cock home. Another orgasm began to build, and she dug her nails into his arms, gasping at the powerful sensations. She climaxed, shaking, whimpering, and satisfied.

Adam walked, still holding her, no longer worried, and laid her on the bed. She was about to climb up higher, but he kept her on the edge of the bed, one knee raised and one foot on the floor. His fingers found her drenched opening, and he coated his fingers in their joint juices. He used them to push into her rear entrance, and she fell forward, all the strength having left her arms. Her mate yanked her back, rough but not painful. His cock head replaced his digits and eased into her ass. His name trembled on her lips, but she couldn't even speak the word, the pleasure was so good. He took her over and over, a strong arm holding her up at the same time he drew her onto his shaft.

Time passed, and the sun dipped below the horizon. Adam's desire seemed not to lessen, but then neither did hers. They stood in the shower and washed each other, made love there, and then ended up back in the bed. Around seven in the evening, Sakura escaped the headiness that was her man and sagged into a chair, naked.

"If we don't stop, we're going to go all night." She looked over at him stretched out on the bed, but averted her gaze from his cock. Her mouth watered every time she saw it, and his reaction to that desire was much worse.

Adam sat up and shook his head, leaning over the side of the bed, as if he could shake off the dregs of lust. ""You're right. Go shower. This time I'm not going with you. I can't help myself. Whenever you get excited, I smell it, and it drives me insane. I don't know how we're going to stay out of bed with this kind of reaction. Not to mention you heal fast, so I can't use the excuse that you're too sore to make my blood cool."

"Yeah, that is weird," she admitted. "But good." She walked over to the bathroom door and stopped. "Adam, thanks."

"For?"

"For never giving up on me."

She shut the bathroom door before he could respond and turned on the shower. A short while later, she was dressed, having cut off his temptation. Well, to a certain degree. He still gave her an appreciative once over because of the formfitting capris and low cut top. They left the hotel to head over to Deveron's company to demand the answers Sakura sought.

Chapter Twelve

Adam started out holding Sakura's hand across the divider as they drove to Deveron's, but as the minutes passed, the more he fidgeted. She chatted nonstop as if she did so to distract herself from the coming meeting or from thinking of her mother. He found annoyance pinched the muscles at his nape and across his back, but rolling his shoulders did not bring relief. Sakura asked him questions, but he provided only a grunt here and there.

From the corner of his eye, he saw how she pierced him with a glare, and then she tugged her hand away. "Well, Adam?" she insisted. "Do you think it's possible or not?"

He had no idea what she referred to. The rumbling bear in his gut seemed to want out, and his control had begun to slip. On top of that, whatever patience he maintained had snapped a few blocks back. "What?"

She rolled her eyes. "Are you even listening to me?"

"No, Sakura, I'm not," he grunted, and her eyes

widened. When the eyebrows furrowed above brown eyes snapping with fire, he knew he'd done it. "*Lo siento.* I don't know what my problem is right now. I can't keep this damn bear down."

No sympathy came his way. "You better figure it out, because I don't appreciate being yelled at."

"I did not yell." He ground his teeth, but when a Walgreen's came into view, he made a beeline for the parking lot and threw the car in park. "I think it's hunger. Hold on. I'm going to grab a snack."

As he strode away, despite the door being closed and the window raised to conserve A/C, he distinctly heard her say, "Is this what I have to look forward to from now on?" He almost grinned, but hunger stirred in his stomach along with an odd itching in his scalp. *Is this what I have to live with?*

Opening the door to the convenience store, he hoped the itching had nothing to do with a transformation, or there were about to be a small crowd of people screaming and running for their lives. Cramped aisles displayed items he had no interest in. He came upon a shelf displaying pastries and spotted honey buns. Was there honey in them? Ignoring the nutrition facts, he glanced around and gave one of the packages a sniff. Very little, to his disappointment, and he confirmed by reading the package that they contained less than two percent dried honey. His ire rose.

What am I doing? I'm human. Grab chips, a soda, and a package of cookies and get out of here.

He gathered the items he had listed in his head and approached the counter, and then held up a finger to the cashier and returned for the buns. Couldn't hurt anything. Before he reached the car, he devoured two of the buns and was about to tear into the sour cream and onion potato chips. The acrid stench of fear overpowered the snack, and he glanced up from them to scan the area. He spotted Sakura, standing beside the car rather than in it, and a man stood beside her watching him.

Adam had seconds to take in the fact that the fear came off this person and that he couldn't see where he had put his left hand—before he blanked. One minute he stood closer to the convenience store than to the car. The next instant, he bore down on the man, sure he had begun to turn. The metallic taste of blood coated his tongue when his canines thickened, elongated, and sharpened to points. Shirtsleeves ripped as his biceps expanded. He curled clawed fingers, ready to rip his enemy to ribbons and opened his mouth to let out a growl fit to make the man piss himself.

Adam raised a hand, seeing the destroyed face already in his mind.

"Adam, no!"

How the hell did he form words? They would not come, but Sakura's warning stopped him cold. He stared at the two of them, from her to the man and back again. Another try produced, "He touched you."

"Only my hair, baby. Not a big deal, okay? We don't want to do this here." The soothing quality to her voice was not her. He didn't like it. She should have already stomped this human into the ground. Adam didn't know he took another, threatening step until she spoke again, trying to get him to calm down.

"W-what is he?" the man stuttered.

"You shut up," Sakura ordered.

The man laughed. "I think you forgot who has the gun, Sakura."

At first, Adam didn't know why, but when the man called her Sakura, it calmed him down. The bear stirred but just a little. His teeth returned to normal, and so did his claws, but he kept his gaze on the man. Once his mind cleared, he figured it out. This was no random mugging. The human targeted Sakura. He knew who she was, but by his stance, the scent of fear, and the way he held his weapon, Adam concluded the man did not work for Sakura's dad. He must have come to kill or retrieve the daughter who had been foolish enough to become one of the enemy.

For a heartbeat, Adam flipped his gaze to Sakura. Her slight nod told him she had come to the same conclusion, and she wanted to see where this led, maybe get a bit more information, like who sent this *idiota*. The second man did not catch Adam unaware. He smelled and heard him coming, but he waited for contact. When the point of a knife touched him mid-back, he stiffened.

"Okay, we're going for a little ride," came the heavily accented English. Adam recognized the Mexican accent. Although the knife cut into his skin, he refused to budge until Sakura got into the car with her assailant in the back seat, still holding onto her hair and pointing the gun at her.

Adam ground his teeth. "I'm going to take the arm in payment."

The man sneered, revealing a garish grill. "*Qué?*"

"You heard me." Adam walked around the car and slid behind the wheel. The second man sat behind him and directed him to start the car. "Where?" Adam demanded.

"Just drive," was the reply. "Southwest One Eighty Fourth."

Adam tightened his hands on the steering wheel. He could guess the next direction. Eventually, they would arrive at the Everglades. Miles and miles to do whatever they wanted under cover of night—well, as long as no one happened upon them before they were done with their business. He knew authorities patrolled as much of the area as possible, but that didn't stop incidents from happening. Adam didn't care. He didn't need long. When he was done, he would feed these men to a croc, and there would be no evidence left.

Adam stopped the car on a lonely stretch of road with only the moonlight and stars to illuminate the night. The man behind him directed him to turn off the headlights. "We don't want anyone seeing what we're up to."

The other man laughed as he exited the vehicle. "These some nice wheels you have here. I'll be happy to take the car off your hands after we kill you."

A bit of gravel or a rock caught under his foot, and he tripped. With a hold still on Sakura's hair, he gave it a yank as he stumbled, and Sakura cried out, raising her hands to her head.

"You dumbass," Sakura shrieked. "Don't you know how to walk?"

The words were the last Adam heard. A roar split the night air, and it took a moment or two to realize the sound came from his mouth. He launched onto the man before anyone could react, including Sakura. He held a scrawny wrist between his jaws and crunched down. The howl of pain only fueled his rage. Adam reared back on two legs and swiped long claws across the man's chest. The jacket, shirt under it, and flesh, all shredded, and the scent of blood filled Adam's nostrils. The man fell down dead on the ground, and Adam swung toward his next prey. The man who'd just finished threatening to kill them squealed like a girl, backing away until he fell on his ass. He scooted along the road whimpering and begging for his life. Adam stalked closer, but Sakura moved in front of Adam and grabbed hold of one of his ears.

"I think you better start talking before I let him kill you," she told the man. "You've already seen what he did to your friend."

The man babbled. Adam gave a half growl and wagged his head, but Sakura held on, giving his ear a rough squeeze that stung. He nosed her leg, but she seemed unimpressed.

"Well?" she demanded, hand on her hip. "Who hired you?"

"*No sé nada, hombre,*" he whined.

"Oh, you don't know anything, huh? Nothing?" She released Adam, and he sprang forward. The man's voice vibrated on Adam's eardrums. He raised a paw. The man shrank in on himself.

"Okay, okay. I'll talk!"

Sakura appeared beside Adam and, without fear, curled fingers over his claws. Adam huffed, and she patted his head. He ducked away but stayed alert. The man stared at him wide-eyed and licking dry lips.

"Go ahead," she prompted.

The man's gaze never left Adam's. "I don't know who she was but—"

"*She?*" Sakura interrupted.

"*Si*, a woman. She said she would pay us good money to get rid of you two." He pointed to Sakura, but when he started to point to Adam, Adam growled, and the man bit his finger as if that would undo the insult. "You and your boyfriend."

"What makes you so sure you had the right target?"

The man dug in the back of his ratty jeans pocket and removed crinkled paper. Sakura unfolded it. She studied the sheet and then held it in line with Adam's vision.

"He even understand?" A nod at Adam.

"Of course."

Sakura refolded the sheet with a picture of herself and Adam, a print-off of a scanned photo, one he knew Sakura kept in her drawer at home. She had never told him about it, but he had stumbled onto it while searching for a sex toy he had brought over for her previously. At the time, the picture confirmed his suspicions of her feelings for him, and he had never told her about seeing it. Whoever entered her house must have known how to disarm the alarm. He knew for a fact her dad had the code.

"So how did this woman contact you? In person?"

"No."

"Phone? Email?"

The man rubbed the back of his head, hesitant. "A

friend of mine did some work for her about five years ago. I guess she still had his number. He said she suddenly called and wanted to hire a couple of guys for a job. We were it."

"F-five years ago?" Sakura sagged into Adam's side, and he easily supported her weight. "A woman. What was her name? Give me something!"

He shook his head. "I swear, man. I don't know nothing else."

"Your friend, then."

The head kept swinging side to side. "No way. I can't roll over on him. You're going to have to kill me."

Sakura blinked at him. "Are you sure about that?"

He shut his eyes, bracing himself. "Yeah."

"One last question," Sakura whispered. "What kind of job did your friend do or hired someone else to do for this woman five years ago?"

"Dumped a body. *Muerto.*"

"Dead," Sakura repeated. "A woman's body?"

"No, a man."

Adam flattened his prey and took his life in one bite.

"I could have beaten more out of him," Sakura said as she drove.

"I was hungry," Adam said.

She screwed up her pretty nose at him in the rearview mirror. He scooted down a little lower on the seat as not to alarm anyone who might happen to glance over and spot a naked man riding around in public. "You didn't eat him, Adam."

"I meant I'd only eaten a couple buns. The bear wanted to kill something. I couldn't stop him."

"You say that like you're two different people."

He sighed, still irritable. "Not people. Anyway, I'm sorry, and you don't seem that upset that I ruined your chance."

"No, I guess because I'm sure the friend didn't dump my mother's body."

"Of course not. There was a closed casket, but she was shipped back to San Diego."

Their gazes met. She shook her head. "I can't speculate about that. I was wondering if you're sure those men aren't going to come back as shifters."

He frowned. "You mean zombie bears?"

"Ugh, sounds like a bad B movie."

He managed to chuckle. "No, dead means dead, shifter or not."

After Sakura retrieved clothes for him from his hotel room, she dumped them in his lap and kept watch while he dressed. He stepped from the car and drew her into his arms, breathing deep to take her in. Her hair tickled his nose, and he remembered that asshole tugging it.

"You're okay?" he asked.

"Yes, for the millionth time, Mr. Obsessive. You actually hulked out just because I had my hair pulled."

"I did not hulk out, whatever that is."

She wiggled out of his arms and walked around the car to the passenger side. "You tore out of your clothes until just threads hung from your massive body. You, sir, hulked out."

"Well, you weren't afraid of me."

"Boy, please, I have my knife right here if I need it. I could have gutted you in a heartbeat."

He eyed her, and she laughed.

"Okay, I saw that you recognized me right away, and I sensed you wouldn't hurt me. What did I have to be scared of?"

"Don't grab my claws like that again. They're pretty sharp."

"*Si, papi,*" she teased, and his cock swelled in his jeans.

What he hadn't counted on was the furnace flaming to life inside him, which Sakura matched. The two of them had enjoyed an hours-long sex session earlier, yet even now as he scented her in his nostrils, it made him hungry for more. Her beauty tantalized him and tortured him, and while taking her slaked his desire, it left him parched as well. Did she realize her power? He didn't think she knew the depths of his need for her, but he intended them to explore together, forever.

With no more delays or interruptions, they arrived at Deveron's company. Tonight, if the lead fox shifter didn't tell them what they wanted to know, he had every intention of beating the truth from the man, and if need be, doing to him what he'd done to the hired thugs earlier. Anything to give Sakura closure and peace.

He pulled up to the guard's box and prepared to explain to the guard why he needed to raise the barrier for his own good, but it turned out to be unnecessary. The man pressed a button to do just that and waved them on. Adam found parking outside the entrance, and together he and Sakura strode inside. Unlike the last time he was there, the place seemed to be a hive of activity, and Adam smelled humans. He eyed Sakura, but she cast him a look that said she had no clue what was going on either.

Deveron appeared from around the corner. "Friends, it's good to see you again."

"When did we become friends?" Adam snapped.

Deveron flashed a bright smile. "We will be. Give it time."

"Don't think I will. Thanks." Adam approached him, wary. "What you're going to do, Deveron, is tell us everything you know."

"Let's find somewhere private, shall we?" Deveron dropped his voice low. "Overtime tonight. *Humans.*"

They were shown into an office this time, and Deveron shut the door behind them. Adam took in the décor. The dark cherry wood furniture and paneling didn't appeal, so he dismissed it all and turned back to Deveron, folding his arms over his chest. "Don't you want your bodyguards with you?"

Deveron waved a hand and took the seat behind the desk. "I don't need them."

"You will if you had anything to do with killing Sakura's mother."

For the first time since they arrived, Deveron sobered. "I'm prepared to tell you everything I know— well, almost everything."

Adam flared his nostrils. *"Everything."*

"You'll be satisfied with what I share. I promise."

Sakura stepped forward, sat down, and crossed one leg over the other. "I'll be the judge of that. We know you and your people were in the hotel room where my mother died. I'm thinking you were there that very night."

"I could have come to do my own investigation," he suggested.

"Did you?" Adam demanded.

Deveron steepled his fingers on the desk, and before he lowered his gaze, Adam thought he saw frustration, anger, maybe anguish in the depths. "No, we were there the night it happened, but I wasn't there to kill her. I went there to kill your father."

Sakura gaped. "You're crazy if you thought that would happen."

He shrugged. "I was more full of myself back then. I—for lack of a more accurate word—*ruled* Miami when it came to shifters. With my intelligence. I got full of myself. I had intel that your father came to town, and I intended to be the one to take him down by my own hands."

"And what happened?" Adam asked.

"We were slaughtered. I was down to a few men, but at last I broke through his defense to where my information said he was. What I found..."

"What did you find?" Sakura insisted, leaning forward. Her pallor seemed too pale to Adam, but he knew to try to get her to calm down now would be futile. Besides, she wasn't so fragile, and if she fell, he would catch her. He took a few steps closer to her and stood guard behind her chair.

"My friend," Deveron said, and Adam heard raw pain. He drew a deep breath and blew it out. His gaze glassed over, and he spun to stare out the window, but Adam doubted he saw anything. Not because of the night, but because he recalled the past. "The humans were all drugged, asleep—the owner, her husband, a few guests. There weren't many. However, the shifters—my people—were dead, their bodies yet to be cleaned up.

"Your father came out of the room on the second level, wild-eyed, manic. I didn't stand a chance. If the two men I had left hadn't come along to create a diversion, I would have died that day. As it was, I got away with my arms, legs, and my stomach cut. I think he got some kind of sick pleasure in slicing me with a sword."

Sakura shut her eyes, head bowed. "A katana. Mama had a thing for all things Japanese for a while. Dad must have used her weapon."

Deveron banged the desktop, and Sakura jumped, opening her eyes to look at him. Adam snarled, daring him with a look to try anything, but he settled back, his shoulders stooped. "I knew I had one friend left other than the two who helped me, but he was dying. I hid and waited. From my vantage point, I witnessed your father shout orders to others and call someone on the phone."

"A cleanup crew," Sakura supplied. "I can't believe he had the presence of mind to do all of that after finding Mom." Her voice held pride and pain.

Deveron looked at her in disgust. "You admire him?"

"Your people killed my mother. I don't care if we slaughtered every one of you. It doesn't equal her life."

Deveron flattened his hands on the desktop and rose in degrees. Adam repositioned himself in front of

Sakura. She stood and moved to his side, no doubt refusing to be cowed by the likes of the older fox shifter.

"Another car pulled up to the motel, and a woman got out. She spoke with your father a few minutes and then went inside the room. He left in another vehicle, along with his men. I was in no condition to attack the woman, not knowing her skill or that of the guards she had with her. Then she called in help, still another vehicle, this time a van. She didn't wait for them or speak to them at all. She left, and the men from the van took my friend away. We followed. They dumped him in a place he would never be found by any human, but we were there. He was almost dead. Five shots to the chest, a slice across his eye."

Sakura dropped to the chair she had vacated. Adam grasped her hand in his. "Savino. That's who you're talking about, isn't it? That big dude who works for you, obedient like a servant?"

Deveron continued speaking as if she hadn't said anything. "I knew the kind of man your father is, and I knew the truth. We withdrew from Miami. In fact, we completely left America. We traveled back to Italy, Savino's homeland, and stayed there for four years. When he was strong enough and agreed, we returned."

"With another plan," Adam said. "To take down her dad."

Deveron shook his head. "I don't have to."

Sakura surged to her feet. "Who gives a crap about your plan? I want one thing only. I want you to bring that no good son of a bitch Savino out here so I can kill him."

"He's suffered enough!"

"Not yet, he hasn't." She pulled her knife from its holder. "I'm going to carve out his other eye before I kill him."

Adam spoke up. "Why did it take him so long to heal? I thought all shifters have a natural accelerated ability to recover."

Deveron shrugged. "Savino has a lot more than you know to deal with, but his inner demons are his own. Either way, he did not kill your mother."

"Deveron," Sakura said, a warning in her tone, and Adam doubted she would hold it together much longer. He laid a hand on her shoulder and felt her pull against it with a strength that far exceeded what she'd had as a human. Still, he hardly flexed a muscle to keep her in place. He had another question, since it was obvious Sakura was too worked up to put together the clues Deveron presented them with.

"Deveron," he said over his mate, "what was the woman's name who arrived at Kasen, Sr.'s calling?"

"I didn't know then, but I learned much later. It's Gladys, your dad's lover and former best friend to your mother."

That's when Sakura figured it out. The same woman who dumped Savino in a place where no human would find him had hired men to kill her and Adam. The coincidence was too great otherwise. The next question was, did Kasen, Sr. order her to do so?

Chapter Thirteen

"Why did she hire lowlifes to take care of the body? Why not leave it to the cleanup crew?" Sakura speculated. "After all, they had other dead shifters. Deveron said so. If he can be believed, that is."

Adam tossed his suitcase on the bed. They had determined it was ridiculous to occupy two different rooms at two different hotels. Besides, when they'd gone back to his, Laila had been there, sexy and kittenish—so unlike her alter ego—waiting naked in his bed. Adam had scarcely been able to control his hellcat at that point. He almost missed what Sakura said, now remembering her leap through the air and the shockingly fast way she'd pulled out her knife and nicked Laila's face with it. On instinct, Laila had hurled Sakura across the room with a strength no normal woman should have. The situation really got out of hand when instinct also kicked in for him—and he had ruined another set of clothes.

Him in bear form woke Sakura out of attack mode, and eventually the women came to an unhappy truce.

Laila would back off and return to Texas, and Sakura wouldn't hunt her down like the beast she was. He still marveled that his mate didn't think of herself as a shifter. Laila had left him with the warning that if he didn't control his emotions, he would end up revealing their existence, and that couldn't happen.

"You don't have to defend her at every turn," Laila said in parting, jealousy clear in her eyes. "This ain't her first rodeo. She's strong enough to take care of herself."

"I know, I know. Hard habit to break. I'm Sakura's protector. Even if she didn't need me as much then and maybe less now, the emotions are a hundred times stronger. I've got her back, and I won't allow anyone to hurt her—even you, Laila."

Laila had threatened something about coming back to warm his bed when he was ready, and he waved her off onto a shuttle to the airport. Then he had spent the rest of the night demonstrating to Sakura no woman could please him like she could.

"Adam Michael Martinez, are you even listening to me?"

He dropped on the bed and lay back, pulling her with him. "Every word, *mami*."

She swatted at him and rolled away to start unpacking his bag.

"I can do that."

"You never unpack. I'll do it. Anyway, I was saying I'm calling my dad and asking him about Gladys. I'm just trying to figure out how to go about it so he doesn't clam up like usual."

"Just come out with it and don't take no for an answer."

"Have you met my father? He can be stubborn."

"Once or twice." He grinned and then sobered. "You think Deveron was lying about Savino?"

She frowned. "I don't know. I kind of think *he* doesn't believe Savino did it, but that proves nothing. He said himself, back then Savino was more a friend than a servant. Deveron was prepared to kill my dad, so it stands to reason Savino would have no qualms about attacking my mother. I mean, she didn't go out on assignments a lot, but she was still a trained hunter."

"True. So?"

"So I want to know why Gladys didn't follow protocol, and then I'm going to learn who Deveron is protecting. If it's not Savino, then I'll find out who it is, and that person is going to die."

He shrugged. "Okay, let's do it."

A knock sounded at the door, and they both said, "Roger!" at the same time.

Sakura started to answer, but he barreled past her and wrenched the door open to jerk the man into the room. Roger's feet dangled in the air, and he offered an ingratiating smile that did nothing to lessen Adam's dislike of the man.

"Why are you here, Roger?" he demanded. "If you still think you have a chance with Sakura—"

"No way, man. I know she's your mate. I'm strictly hands off." He strained to see Sakura around Adam. "Tell him, Sakura."

She studied her nails. "Why should I? You could have been the one to turn me. I might have been a bear like Adam right now."

Adam's eyes widened. Did she really mean she would have liked him to have turned her? Thinking that, his hold on Roger's collar tightened until the man gagged and coughed. Adam eased up. "Again, why are you here?"

"If you let me go, I'll explain."

Adam opened his fist, and Roger fell to the floor. He rubbed his neck and shot Adam a look of irritation. When he stood, he faced Sakura. Mentally, Adam dared Roger to take a step toward her. Roger wasn't such a fool. He remained where he stood.

"Please believe me. I'm not the one that turned you. Deveron's smarter than that, but I couldn't stick around for you two to jump to that conclusion and kill me without questions. Anyway, I think you should call your dad."

"Gee, thanks." Sarcasm dripped from Sakura's words.

"Hear me out. I've been on the scene a lot longer than you think. Remember I told you I travel a lot? Well, I spent a lot of that time in Italy, working for Deveron. That fact wasn't common knowledge when your dad hired me."

"Obviously."

"Deveron tried the physical thing and almost got killed for it, so he decided to use his brain."

"We pretty much got that from him," Adam spat.

Roger folded his arms over his chest. "Did you also know I had contact with Shiya long before she went to Juneau?"

Adam stared. Sakura shouldered by him and grabbed Roger's shirtfront. "You better explain real quick."

"Happy to. I gave Shiya all the information she needed to figure out that Birk was a shifter. I pretty much sent her to Juneau."

Adam ground his teeth. "You're bragging about risking her sister's life?"

Roger held up his hands. "She was never in danger of being killed. We have all the data figured out, and we monitored everything she shared with Birk."

"You pervert!" Sakura drove a fist into his jaw, and Roger hit the floor once more. Adam sighed and reached for his mate.

"Hold on, baby. I think he's got a lot more to share. You don't want to punch his face in before he gets to say it."

"He's filth! He hacked into Shiya's computer, and he sent her to Juneau knowing she could have been killed."

"She wouldn't have. I know it," Roger insisted. "By the time she went, Birk was already half in love with her, and from the signs he gave off, Deveron suspected she was his mate. No shifter has ever murdered their mate. It's not possible. Birk would have died before he let her come to harm. What's funny, though, is with all Deveron's scheming, he never thought Kotori would also mate with her."

"You find my sister's love life funny?"

Roger scrambled back a few steps once he had regained himself. "All I'm saying is Deveron orchestrated most of what happened. We even had a backup for all the data. It was never gone. I know I told you different, but I wasn't ready to tell you everything then. We had to make your father desperate."

"So you could come in all fresh and brilliant to save the day," Sakura quipped.

He grinned. "Yeah, something like that."

"Well, it's water under the bridge. What does it have to do with me calling my father?"

For some reason, Adam tensed. All that Deveron and Roger shared so far blew his mind, but he had a feeling truths a lot more unsettling were about to come out, and he would have to do whatever it took to ensure Sakura came out on the other side unscathed, or nearly so.

"Do you ever have to return to a city or country, Sakura," Roger asked, "after your assignment is over?"

She rolled her eyes. "More times than I care to admit. Often, we get new information about a shifter who moves into an area we just left. Or more often, another seems to spring up in the same family. That's why my father and brother started talking about killing all the members of a family if even one shifter were born among them, even if they are human."

Adam clenched his hands into fists. He had heard of Kasen, Sr.'s and Jr.'s plan and despised it even before he became a shifter. The Keiths had made it a point to protect humans at all costs, but recently because the shifter population refused to be denied, the heads of the family had decided to abandon their principles from generations past. From the first he had heard of it, he had determined to stand in Sakura's way should she dare go that route. So far, she had ignored the order.

"Have you ever had a mission or heard of one of your sisters having a mission in Miami?" Roger asked. "I mean other than five years ago?"

She gaped at him. "No, I haven't."

"And you wouldn't have—ever. As I said, I monitored all of your communications. I even sent a few tips your way to direct you. Every single reference to Miami was wiped from your database the moment it appeared. All tips were ignored and evidence of them destroyed."

She paled. "W-why?"

"Ask your dad."

"You're not going to convince me my father was up to something."

Roger ticked off the points on his fingers. "He lied about the city where your mother was killed. He deleted all references to Miami. You know how you all have kept up with practically everything that goes on in the world. Are you going to tell me he didn't know Deveron was back in the U.S. and living in Miami? The very place one would think he'd monitor because experience dictated more shifters arise in places where they thrived previously."

Sakura sank down on the side of the bed and put her hands over her face. "You're right. I know he was grief-stricken to lose my mother, but this isn't grief. This is suspicious."

"Good. My work here is done," Roger announced. With a cheerful wish that they have a good day, he turned and left. Adam sank beside Sakura and drew her into his arms. She moaned and clutched him tight, but no tears wet her face. He waited in silence, stroking her back until she was ready, and then she picked up her cell phone to dial her dad.

Adam leaned against a wall outside of the room where Sakura met with her dad. Kasen, Sr. rented the mansion and then insisted they meet there. Adam had slipped away while Sakura slept to give the place a once over and to determine that her dad hadn't set a trap. Avoiding the guards since he had no idea whether Kasen, Sr. had given the order to have him killed, he had cased the house and found Gladys, but he hadn't approached her yet. Adam watched the woman with Kasen, Sr. through a window. He heard her words with ease as she comforted him in his agitation about being back in the "hated city."

"Don't worry, honey bunny," she purred to Kasen, Sr., "this nightmare will be behind us soon, and you can have Sakura back home again."

Adam gagged at the endearment and missed Kasen, Sr.'s response. He considered it enough to know the woman who wanted them both dead was in town. They could deal with her later.

Coming back to the present, he listened to Sakura speaking in the other room, her tone deceitfully calm, but he didn't sense her about to fly off the handle. "Dad, I wanted you to come down here because I want you to tell me to my face what happened to my mother. I know she died in Miami and not in Las Vegas, so don't start feeding me a bunch of bullshit."

"Young lady, you will not talk to me that way," was the heated response.

"We're not going riding a merry-go-round, *Daddy Dear!*"

"Sakura, this is my final warning."

Her caustic laughter filled the air. "Okay, I see I'm going to have to be first in laying my cards on the table."

Adam shook his head. He knew what was coming. Sakura intended to reveal the thing Kasen, Sr. feared the most—that he would lose his last daughter to the shifters. Knowing what was coming, Adam turned away and walked down the hall, pulling his cell phone from his pocket as he went. He found a room no human guards occupied, or were close enough to overhear, and dialed the number he had programmed into his phone.

A deep voice sounded across the line on the second ring. "Adam, how's it going outside?"

For a moment, Birk's choice of words threw Adam off, but then he recalled a fact he had learned not long ago about Alaskans. Any other place outside their state was termed "outside."

He shook his head. "Everything is...I guess you can say up in the air at the moment. What I do know is Sakura needs her sister. She needs her family, so I'm calling to invite you to bring Shiya to Miami. It's not any kind of trap. You have my word."

"I'm not worried about that," Birk assured him, sounding amused. "I talked to Laila."

Adam winced.

"She says you're one of us now. I'm glad. What about Sakura? She accept you?"

"Uh...well...we're mated, anyway."

"What aren't you telling me, buddy?"

Adam ran fingers through his hair and paced the room. "She's a shifter."

"That's fantastic!"

"She's not a bear."

The line went silent.

"Birk, are you there?"

"Just what kind of animal is she?"

Adam felt his cheeks warm, and he cursed under his breath. "She's a fox. There's a...clan, group, den? Whatever you call them, down here."

Birk whistled. "Didn't see that coming. Blows my mind."

"Who are you telling?" Adam complained. "So will you come? It's more than just about Sakura's change. She's confronting her father right now about their mother's death. She needs Shiya, and I think Shiya would want to be told everything in person."

"Miami? Kotori and I don't really do warm weather."

"I'll fill the tub with ice for you."

"Haha, funny. Okay, I think you're right. Shiya will want to be there. She misses her sisters, especially now."

"Now?"

"Never mind. We'll come. Give me the address and the name of a good hotel."

Adam studied the room where he stood, one of many lavishly appointed rooms in the villa on Collins Avenue in South Beach. The price had been steep, he knew, at over five thousand dollars a night, but it would house the family.

"We can accommodate you here," he said. "Just come." After he had shared the address with Birk and confirmed Birk would send him a text with their flight information, he hung up and paused. He didn't have a contact number for Shae.

Determining to rejoin Sakura, he left the room and stepped into the hall. At the opposite end, he spotted a familiar face and frowned. He followed the man to a door, which he discovered to lead to an office. He stepped in and shut the door.

"What are you doing here, Roger?" he demanded.

Roger swung around as if surprised, but he knew it was an act. "Me? Don't you know? I'm everywhere."

"If you're plotting for Deveron—"

"No, no. Nothing like that."

"You're still spying for him."

Roger just smiled. He studied the man who should have been a snake rather than a fox. Then a thought occurred to him.

"Do you happen to have contact information for Shae or her mate?"

Roger's eyebrows rose. "Of course. My database is nearly complete."

"I'm guessing the family doesn't have access to this information.

"Of course not," Roger repeated. "Shae and Eiji are ours, even as far away as they are in Japan. If you need the number, I'll be glad to give it to you. I can even give you their address. Anything for you, *amigo*."

"Just the number," Adam snapped. "We're not friends."

Roger laughed and pulled out a small device the size of a cell phone. He punched a few buttons and then rattled off the numbers. Adam dialed them into his cell and stabbed connect. He left Roger probably holding out for a "thank you," but offered him none.

A quick call got him Shae herself, but she refused his offer, explaining she and Sakura had never been all that close. She was busy trying to overcome the cultural differences, not to mention the language barrier, of her new family. Adam thought he heard hurt in her tone and wondered if Shae hadn't been accepted as yet, her presence maybe even resented. She'd been turned to a wolf, and he had heard her mate, also a wolf, was a rarity himself. All the women in his family were wolf shifters but not the men. How odd.

"I can't force you to come," he said, swallowing his anger and impatience, "but think about it. You need Sakura as much as she needs you right now."

"I can guarantee you, Sakura doesn't need anyone," Shae said. "She was always hard and mean. I don't need the attitude. I've had it up to my neck where I am."

"It might seem like Sakura doesn't care, but she does. Family is everything."

"No, Adam. I appreciate what you're trying to do, but I'm out. Tell her I'm sorry."

He ran a hand over his face and sighed. "Okay, well it was worth a try. Good luck with your new life." He knew that last comment had a bit more bite than intended, but he wouldn't take it back and hung up.

Now to see what his little fox was up to.

Chapter Fourteen

Sakura felt weird and natural all at the same time. She stood before her father in all her "foxy" glory, tail swishing, and a little tickle in her whiskers making her twitch her nose. Her clothes were draped in a pile beneath her feet, and when she glanced up at her dad, she met his horrified gaze.

"No," he croaked in a whisper. "Not you, Sakura. Never you."

Now you know my secret, Dad. You can share yours.

She watched his face crumble and tears fill his eyes. Sakura couldn't remember the last time she'd seen him let go so much. No, she did. At her mother's funeral he had wept as if the world had come to an end, and for all of them, it might as well have. Back then they crowded around him, a strong and proud family, drawn together in grief, standing firm in a conviction to rid the world of shifters. Now here she was, one of the enemy, the last of the infamous Keith girls, the one she knew nobody expected to fall from grace. Why not? She was human too—*was* human.

Her dad covered his face and continued to weep. Sakura started feeling sorry for him, hearing his anguish. She worried she had gone too far. She should have said that she was a shifter instead of going right into showing him. As she pondered what to do, the door opened, and Adam stood there staring at her. He hurriedly shut the door and approached her. The way he locked his gaze on her reminded her he had never seen her in this form. She preened for him and saw appreciation in his response. His hand came down gently on her head, and he stroked it. She tried to nip a finger, and he drew back, a low chuckle in his throat.

I'm not a pet, idiot.

He winked.

When she shifted back to human form, Adam positioned himself between her dad and her as she dressed. Being a small animal, she hadn't ruined her clothes like the big bear before her. At last presentable, she straightened and nodded to Adam. He moved aside, and she took a seat on the chair opposite her dad. Her lover joined her, perching on the chair's arm.

This time, Sakura didn't have to push to get her dad to talk. Seeing her change must have broken him, and guilt clogged her throat having gone so far.

"I loved her more than my life," her dad muttered, tears still flowing down his cheeks. He didn't look at Sakura, but rather stared out the window. "We were one person, had been together so long. I thought we would die together old and gray with our grandchildren at our feet."

Sakura flinched, thinking of her vow not to get pregnant. Adam took her hand and kissed it, then held on. She leaned into his side, listening to her dad.

"I killed them all, you know," her dad said.

Sakura froze. "Come again?"

"The men," he said, although it seemed like he wasn't speaking to her. "Not me really. I ordered Kasen to do it, to kill all the men that were here with me in Miami. Not one was to be left alive."

Sakura felt sick. "*Your* men? They were human, Dad. You're telling me you had my brother kill them? Why?"

"Because I wanted no traces, nobody to be able to say what happened. Not even Kasen knows everything. I came here in secret with a team I assembled. When I flew back to San Diego, I gave Kasen a list of who to kill." He had the nerve to smile, but she didn't believe he felt humor or happiness from his actions. "You know your brother, Sakura. Even I must admit, he is a perfect assassin, a cold-blooded killer. He asked no questions but followed through with the order. Afterward, I provided a cover, a botched assignment that never happened. You girls bought it all."

The pity Sakura felt moments ago disappeared to be replaced with disgust. She didn't know the man sitting before her. "They were humans. No, more than that, they were family! Every one of the men was considered to be Keiths, as much as Shae, Shiya, Kasen, and me. You said it often enough, but it was all a lie!"

"I didn't mean for it to be that way, my darling."

"Tell me why," she demanded.

His shoulders slumped, head bowed, he spoke in a

monotone. "I started suspecting your mother was cheating on me a few months prior to her death. Gladys told me some things I didn't want to hear."

"You believed her," Sakura shouted, and Adam squeezed her hand. She scowled at him. "Everybody knew Gladys wanted you from day one. I think she only started working for the family to get closer to you. Mom was always nice to her. I don't know if she ever suspected that hag."

"Gladys had evidence," he stated, "pictures that showed your mom with another man. K-kissing, holding hands." He shut his eyes and swallowed. "I thought…"

Devastated, Sakura worked to calm herself. Her mom cheating? None of it made sense. Her mom and dad seemed like the perfect couple. She didn't recall them ever arguing, not seriously anyway.

"At first I was angry. I was determined to confront your mother, but Gladys convinced me to verify it with my own eyes."

Sakura nodded. "I give her credit for that much."

"I found her in a motel, a place that was beneath her." His gaze met Sakura's, and she saw a crazed light she didn't like seeing. "I gave her the world. She grew up poor in the ghetto. I showed her a better life, good food, travelling all over the world, and she chose to be with *him* in a seedy motel!"

A bit of the sympathy returned for her dad. "Who was he?"

"Scum."

She rolled her eyes. "Can you be a bit more specific?"

"Bove."

Sakura didn't recognize the name, but then she didn't expect to. Adam had stiffened at her side, and she glanced up at him. He had paled, and his eyes widened in shock. As usual, her lover was very perceptive. "What's the first name, sir?"

"Savino. Savino Bove. That was my wife's lover."

Sakura slapped a hand over her mouth and paced the room. Her mind spun a mile a minute. Her heart raced. She felt dizzy and confused. Savino? That giant, scarred, silent man, who was basically Deveron's pet, had been her mother's lover? *No way, no way, no way. Not in a million years!*

"I walked in on them," her father was saying, and for the first time that day she wished he would shut up. "They were in bed together. She made sounds..."

Sakura gagged.

"I think we get the picture, sir," Adam said.

Her dad went on. "That filthy shifter scum had his hands on *my* wife, and she liked it. I put five bullets in him, and still he came at me!"

Sakura stopped pacing and felt for the hilt of her knife but then remembered she hadn't strapped it on again after shifting. The weapon sat on the table near Adam. She never realized how much comfort she drew from holding it in her palm.

"At what point did he kill her?" Sakura asked after she found her voice.

Her dad looked up. "Sakura, my darling, I have to tell you now. I can't hide it any longer. That thing...didn't kill your mother. *I* did."

The room tilted, and Sakura would have hit the floor

if Adam hadn't seen her falling and zipped across the room the catch her. They sat on the floor, Adam holding her so tight, she was sure her ribs were in danger of cracking. She gasped for breath and he loosened his hold, murmuring an apology in her ear and words of love. The pain brought her back from the brink of falling unconscious, so she was able to take in the rest of her dad's explanation.

"Her katana was there, so I decided if bullets couldn't put him down, I would use the sword. I swung at him. He went down clutching his eye. Your mother begged me to stop and listen. She was crying over that…that *thing*. And when I started to run him through with the sword, she did something very stupid." Her dad sobbed again, loud and uncontrolled. "Sakura, I loved her. I would have forgiven her! It was an accident. You have to know that."

He didn't need to say any more. She knew the truth, and nothing between her and her dad would ever be the same. Sakura buried her face in Adam's neck, and he stood holding her. Rather than return to the chair, he kept walking toward the door and carried her up to their room. For the rest of the day and all night, she lay in his arms, crying like her mother had just died. Adam never left her side.

Sakura woke in the early afternoon and tried to remember what day it was. She failed. All she recalled were her dad's words and his admission of guilt. The house lay in silence at first, but then she picked up the sound of a vehicle arriving. Sighing, she sat up, missing Adam.

A hot shower restored some of her energy, but her mood remained low. After pulling on a simple sundress, she dragged her fingers through her hair. Studying her reflection, she thought she could use some jewelry and makeup, but what was the point? At the top of the stairs, a familiar scent tickled her nose, along with two others she couldn't identify. She took one step down and then gasped. Shiya! That was her sister's scent!

Sakura flew the rest of the way down the stairs and all but ran down the hall. Sliding to a halt, she grabbed the doorframe and paused in the opening. Shiya sat on the chair she had occupied the day before listening to her dad confess to murdering her mother. On either side of her youngest sister stood two huge men, obvious shifters and radiating protectiveness that was almost overbearing.

"Shiya," she shouted.

Her baby sister turned from a discussion she was having with Roger of all people, and a brilliant smile lit up the pretty face. *Still the same,* Sakura mused, taking in the glasses and the overall nerdy, innocent look of her sister. She darted across the room and took Shiya into her arms, hugging her tight.

"I heard about Mom," Shiya whispered, and Sakura pulled back. She saw the sadness in the big brown eyes and the glistening of tears. "I'm so sorry."

Sakura pulled herself together and swallowed the emotion. "Don't apologize for him. She was wrong, but he was worse. All this time…"

"Yeah," Shiya agreed. "He tried to cover it up to

make it seem like a bear shifter attack. Can you believe we ate up his lies all this time?"

"It's how we were programmed," Sakura said, bitterness starting to replace some of the pain. "Dad could do no wrong. He was this massive hero in our eyes, carrying on the family tradition."

Shiya held her hand, and they walked together a few feet away from the men. Of course they could still hear, but it felt good to stand alone with just her sister after so long. If only Shae were there too, the mess would be tolerable.

Shiya pushed the curtain aside and looked out the window. Sakura noted the Florida sun beaming down and glanced over her shoulder at the two men, who were obviously Shiya's mates. Both fidgeted a little, pretending they weren't watching Shiya while also seeming to suffer from the heat.

Amusement lit her sister's face, and Shiya said, "Adam, do you mind if we turn the air down a bit more?"

Adam sprang to his feet. "Of course. Sorry about that."

Sakura caught Adam's eye, and he winked. Her heart pounded in pleasure. She was pathetic she loved that man so much. She needed to tell him, and soon. For now, she turned back to Shiya.

"You look good, baby sis. I guess they're treating you right?"

Shiya smiled. "I'm so happy. My life couldn't be more perfect. Well, except for this mess. Adam said Gladys tried to kill you two. What in the world?"

Sakura nodded. "She came to Miami with Dad. You can guarantee I'm going to punish her ass."

"Don't worry about that, Sakura," Roger interjected. She rolled her eyes at him, wondering why the hell he was even still there. He seemed unperturbed by her annoyance with him. "I've already got a contact picking her up. She's going for a little ride."

Sakura's eyes widened, and Shiya made a startled sound.

"You're kidding."

Roger seemed to think it was fine to kill a human if they came against shifters. "She wanted your dad and conspired to remove your mom. When your dad wanted it covered up that she was having an affair with a shifter, he didn't want the cleanup crew to even have a whiff of Savino, so he ordered Gladys to find another way to dispose of the body. Gladys, unbeknownst to anyone but me"—he preened, causing Sakura to roll her eyes again—"had connections here. She used to live in Miami for a while. Anyway, she called in old favors, and well, you know the rest."

Adam added on, "Gladys found out we were investigating the murder. At first your dad kept it secret from even her, but she found out and called in a favor to have us killed. She had no idea we were already changed by then."

"So this is how it is now, huh?" Sakura asked, looking around at them all. "The Keith family is no more, and the balance has shifted toward the beasts?"

"The Keiths are not gone," Adam whispered, coming to stand behind her. He wrapped her in his embrace, and she laid her head against his chest. Shiya looked at her with wide, happy eyes. Sakura flushed in embarrassment. She tried pulling away from Adam, but he wasn't having it.

"You're mine," he growled low in her ear, and a tingle raced down her spine.

A commotion at the front of the house made them all look toward the door as if they could see who it was. Sakura noted the men drawing in deep breaths and recalled how both Shiya's guys were polar bears. She already knew Adam's sense of smell far outdid hers. She glanced up at him, and he grinned, looking proud of himself. Raising an eyebrow, she waited for an explanation, and then heels clicked in the hall, and the door burst open. Her second sister, Shae, appeared there, and Sakura, Shiya, and Shae screamed.

This time, Adam let her go when she charged out of his arms to run across the room and throw herself at Shae. Shiya made it moments after her and threw her arms around both Sakura and Shae.

"My girls, my girls," Shae moaned, kissing their cheeks over and over. "I've missed you two so much." She drew Shae closer and stroked her hair as if she were a kid. Sakura felt a pang of jealousy, recalling how the two of them had always been closer than either had been with her. The distance had been her fault though, since she tended to draw away. She took a step back, smiling, but immediately Shiya took one of her hands, and Shae took the other. They squeezed and drew her close, their heads bowed.

Sakura heard a low swish of sound and peered over Shae's shoulder to find a very silent Japanese man. He was sexy in his build and his intensity, and he stood behind her sister like a sentinel.

Wow.

Shae sniffed, and her man produced a handkerchief, which she took, offering him a glance full of love and adoration. *Hm, getting kind of sugary in here.* Sakura bit her lip, amused.

"When I called Adam back to tell him we'd come," Shae explained, "he told me everything about Dad and Gladys. I just can't believe it. Are we sure?"

"We're sure," Roger said, and Shae took him in, running her gaze from his feet to the top of his head. Roger reddened, and Sakura and Shiya laughed.

"I just wanted you to be prepared," Adam said. "You two had a long flight. Your room is ready whenever you want to get some rest."

Shae thanked him and turned to Sakura. "Wow, girl, I can't believe it. You and Adam? And you domesticated him, too! If I haven't missed my guess, you two are mated, aren't you?"

Sakura felt heat in her cheeks. "I didn't do anything to Adam."

Shiya pinned her with a look. "The man bows at your feet."

Adam appeared offended, and Sakura suppressed a laugh.

"We always said you wouldn't get a man, but Adam… I have to admit the boy's got guts," Shae added.

"I don't appreciate what you're implying," Sakura snapped.

"Ladies, don't argue," Roger said.

"Shut up, Roger!" Sakura told him.

One of Shiya's men walked up, the bigger Native American guy, and slapped a meaty hand down on

Roger's shoulder. Sakura never saw a fox quiver so much, and she and her sisters laughed at him. The depression eased some having her sisters with her, and Shae seemed to forget she'd just taken a trip of seventeen hours from Tokyo to Miami. Sakura and her sisters chose spots on the couch to talk and touch and sigh.

"We're not done," Shae said as they had discussed what their dad had done. "The Keith family is still here. It's in us, the three of us, as it always has been."

"I agree," Shiya said. "Plus our men and…"

"And what?" Sakura prompted.

Shiya touched her belly. "I'm pregnant."

Everyone gasped. Roger raised his hand. "Who's the father?"

Kotori—Sakura had learned the Native American one's name—started for Roger, but the other man, Birk, stopped him. "Calm, down, Kotori. The little fox isn't even a whole meal."

"Hey," Adam quipped, and Birk offered him an apology on her behalf.

"What about you, Shae?" Sakura asked.

Shae put her hand out, and the silent Eiji took it in his. He didn't show much expression, but she sensed his deep love for Shae and was satisfied he would take care of her sister.

"We're going to try, but not yet. I'm still getting adjusted."

Sakura nodded.

"What about you, big sis?" Shiya asked. "Are you and Adam going to try for some rugrats?"

"Never!" Sakura said.

"Yes," Adam said.

Sakura glared at him. "I guess you've figured it out if he hasn't told you. We're two different species. He's a bear, and I'm a fox. I'm not having some weirdo mutant children with the head of a bear and bodies of foxes, or some other strange combo."

"Highly unlikely," Birk commented.

"He's a vet," Shiya supplied, pride in her tone.

Sakura looked at Shae, and the two of them laughed. Shiya smacked their arms, which only made them crack up more. Sakura sighed. Being silly with her sisters felt good, even in the face of what they had learned, maybe even because of it. She didn't realize until she saw them how much she had needed them. For the rest of the day, they sat together chatting, catching up, and discussing plans for the future. Adam arranged for a caterer to come in for meals. Apparently, a house full of shifters—except for Shiya who was still human—took a lot of food. Sakura had decided she wasn't very hungry but went ahead and ate anyway when Adam threatened to take her on his lap and force feed her. The man was getting out of control.

"What about Kasen?" Shiya said, and everyone fell silent.

Their brother was an evil son of a bitch that Sakura never liked very much. She had never let him bully her, but she knew he had tried to do it with her sisters, especially after she started travelling for work and hardly came home.

"He's going to be neutralized," Roger said.

Sakura surged to her feet. "You're not killing my brother, Roger. I don't care who Deveron thinks he is.

You tell him if he even tries anything, he's going to have to answer to me."

Roger held up his hands. "I said neutralized, not killed. Deveron is not trying to run a shifter nation—yet." He smirked. "But you have to admit, Kasen can't keep commanding a bunch of trained killers to knock off our kind."

"True," Adam said, "but we will deal with him, from inside the family."

Sakura smiled at her lover, and he winked. She glanced away from him before he stirred up her libido and the whole damn room knew about it.

"What about Dad?" Shiya whispered.

"He's..." Adam began and scratched the back of his head, a nervous gesture. Sakura realized she hadn't spoken to him about where her dad was. She hadn't wanted to think about him despite her mind being filled with the story he told of her mother's last day on earth. Adam cast her a sympathetic glance, and she knew it wasn't good. "He seemed to get progressively worse with his confession. He might need psychological treatment. For now, I've checked him into a facility for evaluation."

Sakura couldn't believe it. Her dad, the strongest man she had ever known, had snapped. She had seen the beginnings of it at the end of their conversation and wondered if there would ever come a day when he was okay again. Some part of her hoped so while another didn't want to care.

"We'll visit him together," Shae said, and Sakura and Shiya agreed.

Birk strode over and held out a hand to Shiya. She touched fingertips to his palm, and he guided her to her feet. Sakura watched as he drew her gently against his chest. "You need to rest now."

For the first time, Sakura noted the tiredness around her baby sister's eyes and remembered they had had a long flight as well. She stood. "We can all meet back in the dining room for breakfast."

"Sounds like a plan," Shae said. "I'm beat." She stood as well, and Eiji gave a slight bow to them all before escorting Shae from the room.

Birk, Kotiri, and Shiya said their good nights and disappeared, leaving Sakura, Adam, and Roger. Sakura suppressed a chuckle when Adam offered Roger a firm good night. The man at last took the hint and left. When they were alone, Adam drew her into his arms, and they kissed, a caress that was more sensual and loving than erotic, but she sensed his need simmering beneath the surface.

He raised his head and stroked her cheek. "Okay?"

She smiled. "Yes. You did all this for me."

"And for me," he acknowledged. "You all are the family I never had. Besides, I'd do anything for you."

Tears filled her eyes and spilled down her cheeks. She didn't attempt to stop them. "I know. Thank you. It was the best surprise. You're amazing."

"Hm." He wiped her tears until she pulled herself together and then groaned against her throat and nipped it. "Would you like to reward your mate?"

She grinned. "Maybe."

He reached around and squeezed her ass. The desire

she'd fought to keep suppressed came raging to life. From the fire in his gaze, she knew he smelled her want.

"Adam?"

"Yes," he growled in a thick voice.

"Let's go to our room."

Chapter Fifteen

Sakura didn't know what went wrong. Somehow they got distracted, and Adam's hands on her body led to a place she'd intended to explore in private. In a small open room beneath winding stairs, she tried to get out of his arms and lead him to the second floor. Adam had already slid his hand beneath her dress and was caressing her pussy through her panties.

"Adam, someone's going to see us," she complained but not really caring if they did.

"Everyone's asleep," he countered and nipped her shoulder. "I can't make it that far."

She laughed. A push at his chest produced no movement whatsoever, and when he tugged her closer, she felt the thick erection in his pants. The way his cock twitched, no wonder he refused to go farther. Sakura was in the mood to tease him and twisted in his hold until she was free.

"I change my mind," she said, heading away from him. "I'm hungry."

Adam's reflexes were like lightning. His arm shot out, and his fingers encircled her wrist. She stumbled and fell back against him. Another hand came up behind her head and tangled in her hair. He gave a slight tug that produced tingles in her scalp, and his teeth grazed her neck. "I'll feed you."

Her mouth fell open, and she stared at him. "That's not some offhanded hint you want a blowjob, is it?"

His eyes darkened, and she gulped for a second.

"Adam?"

The sound of material tearing caught her attention. She looked down, and her panties fluttered to the floor, strips of cloth. Her heart hammered, and she licked her lips. Adam seemed to take in the sight of the pulse at her throat, and then his gaze shifted to her lips.

"I want you to turn around," he said in a low tone. "Then I want you to open my pants and take my cock out."

She drew in a shuddering breath. Her pussy couldn't get any wetter. When she hesitated to move, Adam tugged again on her hair. She started to raise her hands to his, but he made a small sound in his throat, and she froze.

"If you disobey, you will be sorry." His eyes glittered.

She turned around to face him and worked the button on his pants loose. The sound of the zipper lowering set her blood boiling. Adam responded likewise each time her desire ratcheted higher. She heard his pulse beating erratically and his harsh breathing. The man had gone from zero to sixty in milliseconds. He was a very dangerous beasty.

Even knowing she treaded on shaky ground, Sakura pierced her mate with a steely gaze. "What will you do if I disobey?"

His lips touched the shell of her ear. "I will eat *you* instead."

A ripple of anticipation rolled through her body. "That's a bad thing, how?"

"I won't stop."

Her knees gave, but he held her up. "Take out my cock, Sakura."

She did as he commanded, knowing the man would follow through with his threat. Adam loved the taste of her come, and he could lick her until she screamed herself hoarse. The only times he'd backed off was when she pushed at him, telling him she couldn't take anymore. To go on as long as his desire held, well, she'd be nuts to challenge him on who would give out first.

She reached into his pants and stroked his big cock from the base to the head, marveling at how it had swelled. Hardly able to wrap her fingers around and have them touch, she tried anyway and stared with hunger at the bead of precome on the tip.

"My balls," he said.

She reached lower and teased his sac with her fingertips. Adam hissed between his teeth. He covered her hand with his and held it in place. Gulping breaths told her he was losing it, and soon he would need to get inside her. She loved knowing even as he commanded her, she had some control over him. Adam's desire lay wholly in her, and no other woman could get him to the place he was now with a few simple caresses.

"Want me to suck it, baby?" she asked, cutting her slitted gaze up at him.

Adam raised his attention from what her hands were doing to her mouth, and he pushed two fingers between her lips. "Like this?"

She sucked his fingers, and he growled low in his throat. He pulled back and swiped the moisture across her bottom lip.

"No, that's not what I want," he said.

He released her and walked over to a white leather couch, dropped down on it, and patted his thighs. "Come here, Sakura."

She followed and stopped in front of him. He halted her before she could climb on his lap to run hands up and down her thighs. Holding her dress up, he examined her, and nudged her legs apart. Eyes narrowed on her pussy, he let out another groan.

"Look at all that come," he said. "Sweet and delicious, I could eat you right here all night."

A tremor pebbled her nipples. "Why don't you?"

He shook his head, dropped the dress, and sat back. "Open the front of your dress and take off your bra."

She reached up to undo the buttons and pushed material wide so he could see her bra. Then she worked the straps over her shoulders and down her arms without taking off the upper part of her dress. At last she had the garment removed and dropped it on the floor. Adam sat mesmerized by her breasts.

"Play with them. Pinch the nipples for me."

She did, rolling the tiny, erect buds between two fingers. His bared cock twitched.

"Suck your fingers and then tease your nipples again. Slowly, yes, like that."

Every command she obeyed, performing for him. His next order had her raising her dress to play with her pussy. She stuck a finger into her heat and pulled it out coated with her juices. The following order was to smear the come onto her clit and then pinch and tug it until she brought herself to orgasm. She did and cried out his name.

His hand shot forward, and he parted her folds to watch come drip down her channel. When it topped her inner thighs, he seemed to snap. A swift jerk landed her on his lap. He gripped her waist in a punishing hold, raised her up, and brought her down on his massive cock. She dug her nails into his shoulders and threw her head back. Adam lifted her again and brought her down a little more roughly. Over and over, they repeated the movements until Sakura's head spun, and she keened at having her pussy stretched around his thickness. He drove himself as deep as he could, held her hips down, and ground into her.

"Sakura!" His tone was almost an accusation that she would dare make him this hungry. She encouraged it, grinding on his erection, arching her back, and letting her breasts bounce in his face. His hands flattened on her back to draw her closer, and his lips encircled one nipple. A hard suck sent a pulse arrowing through her core.

"Yes!" She screamed as an orgasm crashed through her system.

She clung to him, trying to get her head together, but an aftershock followed hard on the heels of the previous climax. Adam didn't slow down for an instant. He claimed her body again and again, demanding with his words and his body for more. She reached between them and found her clit to give it a pinch. Powerful sensations of pleasure took her sanity. She whimpered and then felt Adam's hot seed flooding her pussy. She sagged into his chest, panting but then straightened, wanting him to enjoy the view he seemed to love. When he stopped her, she looked into his eyes. Only then did she realize they were not alone.

She glanced toward the stairs and found Kotori standing there. From the confusion in his expression, he hadn't been sure if he should go back up the stairs or continue down as if he hadn't seen them. Shiya appeared behind him and smacked his shoulder. Kotori snapped out of it, and when Shiya took his hand to lead him back upstairs, Sakura saw the distinct bulge in his pants. Her amusement increased when she heard Kotori whisper to Shiya, "You aren't too tired, are you?"

Sakura turned back to Adam. "See what you did?"

His eyes twinkled. "I wasn't the one screaming." He patted her butt, and she climbed off his lap. The feeling of his cock sliding out of her made her moan, and he chuckled. "Don't worry, *pequeño zorro*. I will give you all you want."

Little fox, Sakura thought, translating his words mentally. He wasn't going to let it go. Well, two could play that game. She grinned at him and preceded him up to the second floor to their bedroom. For the rest of the night, this little fox would show her big bear just how much she could do.

"I can't believe he agreed to see us," Sakura said to her sisters.

Shiya and Shae agreed, and she noted the nervousness in her siblings that she felt herself. The coming meeting with Savino would give them final closure, but it scared the hell out of Sakura too. She felt she'd come to accept her mother's choices without blaming her, but what had she been thinking? Was it just lust that drove her to sleep with Savino? All of them knew the risks of dealing with shifter men. They were sexy and feral, one hundred percent Alpha, and from what Sakura saw and her sisters confirmed, excellent in bed.

A few days after her sisters' arrival in Miami, and before Birk and Kotori could reach their limit with the heat, Deveron had finally informed them Savino had agreed to meet with them. Now they sat down in the conference room at Deveron's company because Savino had refused to come to the villa. The men refused to allow Sakura, Shae, and Shiya to go alone, so they waited in the lobby. All Sakura had to do, Adam had informed her, was to call for him, and he would be there. She loved his protectiveness, but really, even with Shiya being pregnant, none of the Keith girls were weaklings.

"Um, Mr. Bove, Savino, thank you for meeting with us," Sakura began.

He nodded. The big man took them each in in turn, examining them with one eye. Her heart ached knowing her dad had permanently injured the man, and each time he looked into the mirror, he would see the evidence.

That is, if he did look in a mirror.

"We, my sisters and I, wanted to talk to you about your relationship with our mother."

"Yeah," Shae chimed in, "basically, we want to know if it was all about the sex or if she somehow cared about you."

Savino's eyes widened, and he clenched his hands on the table. Shiya flinched, and he quickly placed his hands in his lap, probably trying to look less menacing. The door burst open, and both Birk and Kotori crowded the opening, two sets of gazes searching Shiya out. She sighed in exasperation. "I'm fine, guys. Get out of here."

"Two, huh, sis?" Shae said, shaking her head. "I'd have killed one by now." She slapped a hand over her mouth and looked at Savino, but he gave no reaction.

Kotori seemed less than inclined to leave, but Shiya insisted, and he pinned Savino with a threatening look before he ducked out of the room. Sakura had the feeling he didn't go all the way back to the lobby. Maybe they were this crazy because Shiya was pregnant.

As soon as the door shut, Savino spoke again. "I loved her."

"You're not going to convince me she was your mate," Sakura snapped. "She was already married— happily married I might add."

His single eye met her gaze. "If she was so happy, why was she with me?"

"Maybe you forced her!"

"Sakura," Shae warned. "We're here for the truth, right?"

Sakura folded her arms under her chest and compressed her lips. She hadn't expected resentment to rise, but she was determined to shut up and let the man talk.

"No, she wasn't my mate. I never met my mate, and I thought I would never love anyone. When I met Yvonne, I was different, and she was different. I wanted to be with her, and she wanted to be with me. I asked her to leave him for me. She said she couldn't because you wouldn't understand. So we agreed to see each other when we could. If…"

He fell silent, and Sakura knew what he was about to say. If their mother hadn't been worried about what the family thought, she would be alive today.

Shae shook her head. "I don't know. He might have hunted you both down no matter what your decision. I understand loving my mate more than my life, so I can't say you were wrong. If Eiji belonged to someone else, I would take him!"

Sakura blinked at her sister.

Shae looked at her. "What? I'm just being honest."

Shiya spoke up. "What kind of animal are you, Savino?"

He reddened. "A bull."

"Damn!" the three of them said in unison.

Sakura knew what she was thinking and figured her sisters were as well. "Mind out of the gutter, ladies," she teased her sisters.

Shae rolled her eyes.

A thought occurred to Sakura when she thought of what she would do if Laila hadn't backed off. "Why didn't you try to kill my dad later?"

Shiya and Shae gasped, but Savino sat in silence for a long while. He glanced behind him at the window, but no one stood there. She had the feeling he looked for Deveron's approval. The man should be free of whatever hold the fox leader had on him, but Savino's next words cleared up the mystery.

"I can no longer shift," he said. "I am physically stronger than a human man, much stronger, but I cannot shift. You might have heard it took me a long time to heal from my injuries, much longer than normal. It was because I can't forgive myself for being the cause of Yvonne's death. She… I loved her."

Shiya wept, and Shae hugged her. A lump of emotion rose in Sakura's throat. She felt for this poor man who had suffered so much. Sure he lived after almost dying, but he continued to suffer every day. Losing her mother had broken him, and they weren't even mated.

"Did you turn my mother?"

He shook his head. "I could have, but unless she chose to be my mate, I wouldn't have."

"I'm so sorry, Savino," Sakura said. She reached across the table and touched his hand. He flinched but didn't pull away. "If you ever need anything, please don't hesitate to call me. I'll do whatever I can. I promise you that."

Her sisters echoed the vow, and she spotted moisture in the bull shifter's eyes. He bowed his head. "Thank you. I am happy living a simple life in Deveron's service. I don't need anything more, but I'm glad I was able to meet my Yvonne's daughters. You all three have inherited her beauty, and make me feel like I got to see her one more time."

Each of them gave the older man a hug, which he accepted awkwardly. Then they said their good-byes.

Sakura would do all she could for him and demand Deveron treat him as more than just as an employee. She intended to keep in touch, and maybe by some miracle and with time, Savino's broken heart would heal. That was the least the Keith family could do.

She and her sisters left Deveron's company to return to the villa with their mates, Sakura knowing her sisters felt as she did that she was fortunate to have the man she loved and who loved her still by her sister, for now and forever.

Epilogue

Sakura screamed, but this time it had nothing to do with pleasure and everything to do with pain and panic that she was giving birth. The estimated eight-pound baby was ripping his way out of her womb, and she had already told Adam more than once he would pay with his life.

Miserable, her husband stood by holding her hand despite how she'd tried her best to break it, blaming him for this craziness. "It's okay, Sakura," he soothed. "It's almost over, and our son will be here with us."

"I can't do this," she shouted. "I can't! It's too much. I want more drugs!" She thrashed on the bed, or tried to. All energy had been sapped, and she didn't think she had it in her to push even once more.

"The drugs don't last, baby," he said, almost sounding like he chanted it. He probably did because she had demanded something to soothe the pain for the last umpteen hours. After the initial epidural, which lasted all of a half hour because of her ridiculous healing ability, she was left to suffer. Why the hell couldn't the healing take care of all this pain?

"You're going to pay for getting me pregnant! You hear me, Adam?"

"Yes, Sakura. I hear you. You've threatened castration a hundred times."

"Are you getting impatient with me?" she shouted. "You are, aren't you?"

"Never, baby. Shh, it's fine."

On and on she argued with him until the tiny voice of Adam Michael Martinez, Jr.'s voice echoed around the room. In an instant, Sakura's mood lifted, and the pain eased. She stared in wonder at her little one. After he had been cleaned up and handed to her, she couldn't resist opening the blanket to check him over. Beside her, Adam chuckled.

"Looking for mutation?" he teased.

She glared at him. "You're not off the hook, buddy." Then she smiled, her chest constricting. "Thank you for him, Adam. He's perfect, isn't he?"

"*Si*, just like you, *mami*." He kissed her lips, and weariness had her eyes fluttering closed. The next time she opened them, she was in a different room, and Adam paced at the foot of the bed holding their son and singing to him something in Spanish. Tears flooded her eyes. *Look at me with all this emotion. Get a grip, Sakura.* As much as she lectured herself, her heart still swelled as she watched her family. She'd given in to Adam and married him, pretending at first she did it for him. Her sisters had teased her that no woman's face shown as much as hers when she spoke her vows. She'd threatened them all, but that had made them laugh harder.

A knock on the door turned her attention there, and in walked Shiya holding her twins' hands. The two toddlers, one boy and one girl, each had a lollipop stuck in their mouths. They ran over to the bed and were about to hop onto it when Kotori appeared and calmly scooped the two into his arms, a stern expression on his face. Sakura had heard from her sister that the boy was Kotori's, and the girl was Birk's. She'd asked how they knew and was told it was all in the scent. Yet, from the look of it, they were all one happy family, and the kids considered both men to be their daddies.

Kotori muttered his apology for the disturbance, kissed her forehead and the baby's, and then left with his children. Shiya sat down beside her and hugged Sakura. "I heard from Shae."

Sakura sat straighter. "How are they?"

Shiya sighed. "Shae has too much mouth for her in-laws, so Eiji moved them to a house in Tokyo."

Sakura shook her head. "I don't blame her though. She finally got pregnant, and I know for myself those hormones go whackadoodle. She hasn't adjusted to the culture over there, so I guess being four months pregnant didn't help."

"Please," Shiya said. "She's not trying to adjust. Shae's getting antsy. How much you want to bet Eiji's going to bring her back to the U.S. before the baby's born?"

"Probably," Sakura agreed.

"She said she wanted to wait to get pregnant, but these damn shifter men have super human sperm."

"You should know." Sakura laughed, and her sister smacked her arm. "I know what you mean. I said I wasn't having any, and then this one"—she glared at Adam, but he seemed oblivious playing with their son—"got me knocked up before I knew it."

"You'll have another one by next year."

"Not if I cut off Adam's balls."

This time her husband paled, and she and Shiya laughed.

"I'm pregnant," Shiya moaned.

"You're lying!"

Shiya shook her head. "Nope."

"Wow, your little ones aren't even two yet, Shiya."

"I know. Stepladder kids like us."

Sakura looked at her sister and grinned. "Your crazy behind is happy about it. I can see it in your eyes. You know it's likely you'll have another set of twins, right?"

Shiya grinned. "Yeah."

"What about the obvious question?" Sakura asked her.

"What?"

Sakura hesitated. "Are you going to get turned? I mean, I know they can't do it, but what about another shifter?"

Shiya opened her purse and pulled a sheet of paper out. She unfolded it and smoothed it before handing it to Sakura. A list of names, addresses, and phone numbers extended down the page.

"This is a list of shifters, all bears, different kinds. Two are polar bears."

"No way. Where did you get it?"

"Where do you think?"

"Roger," Sakura answered. "That man is something else."

"Yeah, I discussed it with the guys, and we agreed after I give birth to start the process of finding the right maker."

"Wow, that's awesome. I'm… I don't know. I guess I'm glad for you. I've come to accept what I am, even embrace it. Adam and I are closer, and it feels so good sensing him, knowing how he feels, and being connected to him. I know you'll experience an even greater closeness to Birk and Kotori."

A tear slid down Shiya's face, and she nodded. "I can't wait. I felt like the oddball, but now I'm going to be one of you."

"You were always one of us, baby sis. We love you."

Shiya sniffed. "I love you, too. Okay, well let me get out of here and let you get some rest. I'll come by the house in a couple days to visit with you and my new nephew."

She kissed Sakura and Adam, and then snuggled with the baby, cooing to him. When Sakura was alone with Adam, he returned to her side and sat down. Sakura looked into the face of her sweet baby boy and noted how much like his daddy he looked. "Is he really okay, Adam?" she worried.

"Yes, he's fine, Sakura."

"You're not just saying that?"

He shook his head and leaned down, breathing deep with his nose to the tiny chest. "Not only do I smell my scent and yours on him, but I smell the bear."

Her eyes widened. "So he's a bear shifter?"

"Looks that way. If you're jealous, we can go again and try for a fox."

"Boy, don't even imagine touching me for a while!"

He laughed and appeared depressed, and she stroked his cheek. "Not too long. Don't worry."

He grew serious. "Sakura?"

"Hm?"

"I was thinking of taking a position with Deveron."

She stiffened. "He wants to use you, Adam."

"Baby, it's not like I won't get paid well or that I'll be a lackey. He's offering partnership, and I'll be doing similar work to what I did before as your protector."

"Except you'll be the hunter, chasing down shifters who threaten to expose our existence or who hurt humans, and we're not hurting for money."

"I know, baby."

"It's dangerous," she said.

"You didn't think so when you were out in front."

"It's not that I'm against it." She sighed, and he laid the baby in the bassinet then took her hand. She laid her head on his chest and shut her eyes. "I don't like feeling this vulnerable. I love you so much and little Adam. If I were to lose you…"

"Shh." He stroked her hair. "You're not going to lose me. I'm going to continue my training, and with Roger's intel, much more advanced than what was available in the family, I will have an advantage."

"I know." She sighed. "Look how he was able to pinpoint where Kasen was."

"Exactly. Now your brother is under constant watch. That was all handled without any violence, right?"

She rolled her eyes. "I don't think he had much of a choice when you and my brothers-in-law threatened his life if he ever harms another shifter."

"He will never love our kind," Adam agreed. "But as long as he worries about his own family, he won't make a move against us. The mental break your father had and discovering his involvement in helping to cover the truth also got to Kasen. He's not exactly reformed, but I believe he won't cause any more trouble. So, how about it? Do I have your blessing with the job?"

"Will it mean we have to relocate to Miami?"

"No, we can stay here in San Diego if that's what you want. I already let Deveron know your happiness is more important to me than anything else. If you don't want me to do it, I won't."

"You're sweet, but I won't stand in your way."

He kissed her lips. "Are you sure?"

"Yes, I'm sure."

"So, what do you think about a daughter?"

"Imma kill you."

He burst out laughing, and Sakura joined him, happier and more satisfied than she had ever been. The pain of losing her mother the way she did was still there, but with each passing day, she appreciated the good in her life, like her sisters and their mates, her perfect husband, and now her sweet son. Plus, Savino didn't know it, but she intended to make him honorary granddad very soon, just one more step in restoring a very special soul. She couldn't ask for more.

The End

About the Author

Tressie Lockwood has always loved books, and she enjoys writing about heroines who are overcoming the trials of life. She writes straight from her heart, reaching out to those who find it hard to be themselves completely no matter what anyone else thinks. She hopes her readers enjoy her stories.

Visit Tressie on the Web at
www.tressielockwood.com
or on her blog at
tressielockwood.blogspot.com.